# Shock Totem ₃

## CURIOUS TALES *of the* MACABRE *and* TWISTED

PUBLISHER/EDITOR
*K. Allen Wood*

ASST. EDITOR
*John Boden*

ASST. EDITOR
*Nick Contor*

NONFICTION/SUBMISSIONS
*Mercedes M. Yardley*

SUBMISSIONS
*Sarah Gomes*

LAYOUT/DESIGN
*Rex Zachary*

COVER DESIGN
*Mikio Murakami*

Established in 2009
**www.shocktotem.com**

ISSN 1944-110X

Printed in the United States of America.

# Notes from the Editor's Desk

Welcome to issue #3!

I think you'll like what follows—at least after I blather on a bit. I'll make it quick. Promise.

So our third issue. On time! After everything that happened—or to be more accurate, *went wrong*—between our first and second issues, we put a lot of hard work into getting this one out on time (though let's hope I don't eat those words, considering, at the time of this writing, it's a cold evening in November) and making it bigger and better than before. The latter we achieved—this issue is our biggest yet!—but whether or not it's better is up to you, the reader, and your particular—and hopefully varied—tastes.

Because we've got variety aplenty.

How about a new short story from the black-humored Godfather of All Things *Right* with Horror, **John Skipp**? I can't imagine you've read anything like this one before. How about a tale from **Joseph Morgado**—told in second-person! Go on, roll your eyes; it is, after all, the universal response to such a thing (not to mention usually justified). But this one is different. Give it a chance; I think you'll be pleasantly surprised.

Take a ride with Ed K.

Stroll down Duval Street.

Run through the meat forest.

Seek out ghosts at the old farmhouse.

This issue is full of fantastic fiction from many of the genre's up-and-comers: **S. Clayton Rhodes, Tim Lieder, Amanda C. Davis, Aaron Polson,** and many more. Nonfiction is once again presented by that foxy gal **Mercedes M. Yardley**.

We also have interviews with bizarro heavyweight **D. Harlan Wilson** and **Count Lyle**, lead singer/guitarist of the brilliant **Ghoultown**. Both very cool cats.

And we have some firsts…

Throughout 2010 we hosted bi-monthly flash-fiction contests. Each was a unique prompt-based contest where participants had just one week to write and turn in their entries. From there, each participant, save a few, read the stories and voted for their top three—and most gave invaluable feedback on each story, ensuring that everyone came away a winner on some level—and the First-Place winners received a prize, such as a novel, anthology, a magazine or two. In November, fellow writer and friend **Jeremy Wagner** acted as guest judge. He went through the winning stories and picked an overall winner: A fine little tale from **Steven "Seven" Pirie**, which can be found in this issue.

Also in this issue, the first installment of *Bloodstains & Blue Suede Shoes,* a new collaborative series between our very own **John Boden** and UK-based—and tattoo-covered—writer **Simon Marshall-Jones**. Each forthcoming installment will focus on bands and musicians and music genres—even individual songs—that call upon the darker side of subject matter. It should be a good ride.

And I think that'll do it.

As always, Dear Readers, my staff and I wholeheartedly appreciate your continued support of *Shock Totem* and its authors.

Dig in and enjoy!

K. Allen Wood
November 15, 2010

# Contents

# *Editorial*
# VICTIM OF CHANGES
### by K. Allen Wood

If you can't change something, then change the way you think about it.

I learned that axiom early in life, as a young boy powerless against a dark tide that swept away everything that I held dear. It wasn't until I was an adult, however, that I truly understood the verity of that simple statement.

But this editorial isn't about my stunted childhood or things quite so dramatic. Precisely the opposite, in fact. It's about growing and shifting perspective and being open to change, especially that which cannot be stopped.

To be more precise, this is about electronic publishing.

Ten years ago, give or take, I righteously refused to accept the so-called digital revolution that was battering the foundation of the music industry. It was that dreaded tide again, creeping inexorably closer; but this time I knew its intent, and I stood defiant against it. As a longtime musician and music fan with a collection that rivals that of an indie record shop, I simply couldn't entertain the thought of *owning* anything that I couldn't touch. It's a tragic notion: You can have it, but you can't touch it.

So I planted my feet firm, chose the side of the righteous, and declared the existence of digital music to be a fad. Just another form of media with a little buzz behind it to make people stop and listen for a moment, but ultimately destined for the Halls of Failure, right alongside the MiniDisc, the LaserDisc, and Corey Feldman.

Foot, meet mouth. *Nom nom nom.*

Despite my protestations, along came sites like MySpace and MP3.com, which offered bands and musicians a free platform to release their music—digitally. Eventually, these sites incorporated ways for bands to offer their songs or albums as pay-per-download. You could buy one song, two songs, five songs, the whole album. But you'd never get a physical copy.

The good news (from a purely selfish fan standpoint) was that, at the time, this didn't work too well for bands. I saw it as a sign of failure, indication that the nuisance that was the digital-media craze was dying its unavoidable death, that things would return to the way they had been.

But the good news was also the bad news. So-called fans had quickly learned that digital media could be obtained for free, if one knew where to look. That, of course, was an act as simple as opening your eyes. The craze did not go away, as I had expected and hoped; instead it spread far and wide, across the globe, carried by the fart winds of Al Gore's damnable Internet.

I was not pleased.

Soon after, the once indomitable walls of the music industry began to crumble, and with it, my defiant resolve.

Cut to today, and the music industry is nothing like it was just a few years ago, let alone ten or fifteen. Countless bands have taken control of their own music—and destiny—relying on new technology to get their art into the "hands" of listeners, all without the help of the big bad music industry. Not always a good thing, of course, because quite often—this being both sad and ironic—these bands charge *more* money than any record label would ever have charged, and for a lesser product, usually in the form of a doomed-to-not-play-in-three-years CDR in a cheap cardboard sleeve.

But that's a rant for yesterday. The point is, things changed right before my obstinate stance. I could take my bitter cookie and go home, nibble on it in a dark corner and weep for the return of the good old days, or I could take a deep breath, clear my head, and approach it from a different angle.

Today, I own a Creative Zen 30GB MP3 player—which holds roughly 7,000 songs—and I love it. I spent over a year slowly ripping the nearly 8,000 CDs in my collection (yes, I know that's ridiculous) to a 1TB external hard drive. I have enough music for around 250 days of 24/7 playback—and I love it! I've even bought numerous digital releases, but mostly those with digital-only availability, or as in some cases, a bonus track otherwise only available on the expensive import. I don't love that so much, but if that's the only way to get it, I'm content to accept it. Hell, I installed iTunes!

The music industry has changed, and so have I. Rather, I look at the changes that have gone on within the music industry from a different, clearer perspective.

Which brings me, at long last, to the publishing industry. It's also changing, as everyone knows. What the music industry began to go through more than a decade ago, the publishing industry is going through now. I'd love to rail against the tide of technology and rant about e-books and e-readers, but I know it's pointless. I can't stop it. Neither can you.

The good thing is that books, like CDs—and even the vinyl record, which has seen a steady growth in popularity among the younger generations over the last decade—will not disappear in our lifetime, despite some literary prophets predicting, by way of divine baloney, its sooner-than-later demise.

Though I long for the days when the *physical* medium reigned supreme, and will always opt for real, tangible books from my favorite authors, I've embraced the digital side of publishing. No fuss. No protest. Nada from me. Because like the MP3 wasn't *the* future of music, I know the e-book isn't *the* future of publishing (not anytime soon, anyway). The e-book will, however, be a big part of it—and hopefully, for the sake of the industry and its artists, not as easy to "steal" as music files.

Either way, I'm on board.

This past October, Dean Koontz released a digital-only novella called *Darkness Under the Sun,* a sort of prequel to his novel *What the Night Knows*—which, at the time, hadn't yet been released. I was excited. Despite Koontz being my favorite author, I hadn't giddily anticipated a new Koontz release for a long long time. Not because I like him any less; I've simply become accustomed to his clockworklike publishing schedule. Just like I know there will be a new Terry Brooks novel every fall. It's the nature of the business for novelists, but when things get predictable it tends to rob the reader of that exciting sense of anticipation and mystery.

*Darkness Under the Sun,* however, was a departure for Koontz; it was new territory for him, therefore new territory for me as well. And I was excited.

I now own a Kindle. And guess what? Yep. I love it. Since it arrived, I've downloaded and read *Ur,* a novella by Stephen King, written exclusively for the Kindle and which uses a pink Kindle as the main plot device. I've also downloaded the complete works—novels, essays, short stories, poems—from Poe and Lovecraft, both totaling less than five dollars. I've downloaded—legally—twenty or so classics for free; some of my childhood favorites, like *The House on the Borderland,* by William Hope Hodgson, and *The Empty House,* by Algernon Blackwood. I have a few other freebies on there as well, plus some small-press releases, like the three most recent issues of Apex Magazine. All housed in a tiny-little gadget, with room for thousands more.

Technology is both scary and amazing.

Scary because it can so quickly and effectively change entire industries, thus lives, as we've seen with music and are seeing now with publishing, and amazing for those very same reasons.

Take *Draculas,* for instance, a collaborative Kindle-exclusive novel written by J.A. Konrath, F. Paul Wilson, Blake Crouch and Jeff Strand. I bought it for $2.99. Not a bad price for an e-book. But in addition to the novel, there are perks you will never find in a print edition: An interview with all four authors where they discuss the writing of *Draculas;* scrapped scenes and two alternate endings; "Serial," a short story written by Crouch and Kilborn; "Cub Scout Gore Feast," a short story written by Kilborn and Strand; and yet another short story, "A Sound of Blunder," written by Kilborn and Wilson. Then there are author biographies, bibliographies, excerpts from the authors' other works, and a collection of over seven hundred e-mails which gives the reader—or aspiring writer—an extensive and informative behind-the-scenes look at the writing process of *Draculas.*

For $2.99.

Will all e-books give the reader this much? Probably not. But it's *possible.* Of course, it's possible with print books as well, but hardly practical. That's the key difference. E-books have opened the door to a realm of possibilities previously unheard of—or at least unthinkable.

Stephen King and Dean Koontz are already testing the waters with exclusive material, and the aforementioned *Draculas* showcases in a big way just a tiny fraction of what's possible—and inevitable—in the future. In time, authors will utilize this technology and others to change the way stories are told: There will be audio and interactive video; there will be tie-in stories, like Koontz's novella; there will be interactive tales that put the reader right into the story, making them an active participant in how it all plays out. The possibilities are endless, and I foresee great things to come.

Many of you who read this will shake your head, declare me a loony, and insist you'll never touch an e-reader or read an e-book. Some of you will stay true to that sentiment.

But I find this to be an exciting time, as a writer and a reader, and I've embraced it wholeheartedly.

Yes, it's a fact—e-readers don't look or feel or smell like *real* books, but remember this simple truth: The story is what matters most, not the manner in which it is delivered.

At least, it should be.

# Bop Kabala and Communist Jazz

### by Tim Lieder

I met Ed K. in circumstances of glorious abandon. I was in a supermarket outside Hibbing, smoking Camels. I asked him for change and he blessed me with Marxist doggerel. I thought he was Chinese, but he said he was Korean. The next time I saw him, he was playing a tenor saxophone in a church near Brainard. He squeaked and squawked. His rhythm was spotty. His tone was weak. Ed K. was a convert to the road, to the life, to the random eventuality.

I'd see him many times afterwards, always in extreme unexpected places. I'd go to a Russian tea room with a girl that I couldn't stand. Ed K. would be at the next table playing chess. I'd find myself at an after-hours party in a bar catering to fraternities and Ed K. would be hitting on the blond waitress with green streaks in her hair. I was once in Chaska selling hot dogs from a push cart and Ed K. came up and stole one. He even dated my cousin. My old college roommates loved him; he had been their main supplier.

Ed K. smoked too many cigarettes and drank too much coffee. He was tall for a Korean. I think. When he wore leather, he owned it. When he wore a suit, it wrinkled around his arms; made him look cheap. There were weeks when he'd push the macrobiotic vegan diet. Other times he'd pull the mandatory 28 days. He was Ed K., the musician, the poet, the prophet, the Communist, the seeker, the drug addict, and the preacher.

His preaching ultimately brought the trouble. After I'd known him for a year, I was driving him to preaching gigs in Stacy, Sheboygan and Nimrod. I felt obligated because I was in his car outside Stevens Point, Wisconsin, when he wrapped it around a flag pole. Long story, and you don't want to hear it, but I was in the back seat fighting and fucking Virginia. She's married now. I hear she's happy. I can't say if he crashed it when we were fucking or fighting. Probably the former because I bit Virginia's tongue.

After he lost his license, it didn't take much for him to convince me that sin atonement was predicated on serving Ed K. I didn't mind. Truth is, I was curious. I didn't even know about his preaching before I became his driver. He never told us about his Jesus life when he was rambling fantastic on Aleister Crowley and Karl Marx.

Ed K. had a talent for compartmentalizing. He could hang out with the goth-punk beat crowd in the West Bank, smoking and drinking cheap wine, just after he told a congregation of well-meaning farm folk that hell awaited everyone. Don't think that he was missionizing to the punks, either. He was scoring drugs and fucking Wanda and Jenny just the same as anyone.

He liked to preach in a faraway Assemblies of God church because they still called him exotic. He was about as exotic as chicken chow mien. That Sunday, he had a kimono in my backseat. He was wearing blue jeans and a t-shirt espousing a positive Christian message. It showed off his tattoos.

Many Sundays, he'd finish preaching in Stacy and tell me to drive him to Nimrod for the late services. Then his friends from the Christian Academies would invite him to free verse Christian mission bop sessions.

He was intense about it. The first time I drove him, he stayed silent in the car. From the first hello to the last thank you, he didn't say a word. I can't tell you about his sermon. I waited outside. The second time, he was the same, except I went inside and heard him. He preached hellfire and Jesus.

By the third drive, I said something innocuous like "Nice weather" or "So what are you preaching about?"

"Just drive and shut the fuck up," he said. I shut the fuck up. I knew better than to interrupt Ed K. when he was quiet. He was the talker and when the words disappeared, you couldn't fill the silence with chatter. On the way home he said a few words about the sermon.

~

I know you read the papers and I know what you think happened. You can't believe that garbage. That Sunday was quiet. Peaceful. She appeared on the side of the road like a banshee. She was standing on the shoulder with her thumb out, holding a small bag in her left hand. Her face was squinting and frowning. She was wearing a red checkerboard dress under a German Army jacket. She had tied her long red hair back. I didn't know her name was Mary Abigail Gunderson until I read the papers.

She grinned at our car like she knew we were going to pick her up. Maybe she had been grinning like that all day; the smile made my hands sweat. I hated her on sight. Ed K. told me to stop.

"No," I said.

"Stop this fucking car or I strand you in Stacy."

"You don't drive."

"Brother O'Connor drives and always wanted to drive a Ford."

"No one wants to drive a Ford," I said, but I was slowing for her.

When Mary ran to the car, she was full of "thank you" and "it's so nice of you"; pitching her voice up to cheerleader. She touched Ed K. on the shoulder and she almost kissed me. I smelled her vanilla perfume and I wanted to break her beaky nose. She thanked us again. She slid back on the brown seat and wiped her mouth with her sleeve. She was a tall girl with large arms and breasts that no dress could hide.

I gave Ed K. a bewildered look but he just put his head forward and scratched that space near his cheekbone; the one he could never shave right. For the next twenty minutes, Mary remained silent. The radio played an angry R&B song that didn't make sense on a lonely country road.

I drove under the speed limit. Ed K's midnight poetry baked in my head. The church loomed on the next horizon. I was becoming a good God-fearing Christian. If they wanted me to donate money to fetuses, coming out of homosexuality funds or missions in India, I'd be cool. I didn't need to stay in the car. I could go inside. I could clap. I could sing. I could throw a dollar bill into the hat and shout "Praise Jesus" with my hands dancing and my eyes closed. I was hiding the porn-loving, pot-smoking, whore-renting fucker from Minnetonka. I was a clean boy, just a little rough around the edges. Not all my tattoos were Jesus, but I was Ed K's bud, homie, dude—all the cool words that Ed K's flock used on me.

We drove for just over twelve miles before Mary opened her mouth. I jumped a little when she spoke. I had been getting into the road, working the road, making the road my friend. I guess I had stopped believing in Backseat Mary.

"So, you guys fags?"

"No," said Ed K.

"Okay. It's cool if you are."

"No. It's not," said Ed K.

"Sure it is."

"It's a sin."

"Suit yourself."

I saw the red on Ed K's face and I needed to lighten the mood, but I was empty. Had we been going the other way, her question wouldn't have stung. I was hoping that her words didn't inspire him. It was a hot day. I didn't want to sit in the back of a church listening to Ed K. give his Dead Fag sermon. I had heard it twice before. I was hoping for Jesus Punk. I could listen to the Punk Jesus one for hours. Hell, I could even tolerate a Hippie Jesus sermon. Anything but the Dead Fag one.

Mary was lapsing into a hopeful silence; looking out the windows. She was young but she knew enough to shut up. She flipped her hair once but it was affecting. She was a hip little redhead with a face that said "Yeah I fucked him, what's it to ya?" The happy, grateful Mary was losing ground to the angry, nasty little bitch.

"Stop here," she said. The roads stretched out empty, save for the dead rabbits. Rows of wheat surrounded us.

"Here?"

"Yes. Here."

I looked at Ed K. Ed K glared at me. I didn't stop. Mary was going to church whether she liked it or not. The preacher groove was on and Ed K. never let any cute redhead fuck with Jesus.

"Here!" she said again.

"He has to slow down," said Ed K. His voice was tough. No church was going to take his anger. Hell was bopping. Rage was hopping. We were speeding.

"Shut up, fag!" she said, as if she were joking. Her voice pitched up higher. Ed K. never hit women, never thought of hitting women. Ed K. was a talker, but Ed K. was going to say something. Something bad. Something that would turn that beautiful spring morning into a gray day at the Laundromat.

I'm telling you everything so you know why I gunned the engine. I liked Ed K. He was my best friend, and I wasn't going to start hating him just because a creature of destiny taunted us. I heard her screaming. I stifled a laugh. Ed K. drummed "Wipe Out" on the dash board; the engine was cranking. I smelled cow shit.

"My boyfriend is going to kill you when he finds out about this."

"Relax," said Ed K.

"You know this is kidnapping, right? You know that you're in big shit if anyone catches you, and I will..."

She trailed off, but not because Ed K. was snapping his fingers. I think she realized what she was telling us.

"Please," she finally said, "please don't make me miss him. He's going to be mad if I don't get to the diner on time."

"Then he's going to be mad."

"You don't understand."

I was trying not to talk. The road was throwing up church signs. Two miles away. Little Mary would have to walk. I smiled teeth into the rearview mirror.

The sun was clinging to the interior, washing us all in yellow. The sky was shimmering baby blue like a sweater from 2002. I bopped my head pretending that I trusted Ed K. She was yelling and then she was crying. I turned up the radio. Girl singers were giving their lives to Christ.

I pretended that Mary was someone else, doing something besides sitting in my backseat calling me a faggot. She was holding a large green canvas bag and I understood that bag. Mary Jailbait-girl was running off, packing what she could carry. Her boyfriend was going to be in trouble if anyone talked to the police. I should've thanked her for making my Sunday so joyous. She had her thing going. Going the way the things go. You know what I'm saying. Don't pretend you don't.

Then she stopped. I didn't know if she was giving up or acting petulant. Ed K. laughed. He took all the misery of the drive and buried it under a chuckle. The radio screamed something fat, mean and desperate. Hey. Hey, you. It's all just a fucking dream.

"Tell me about your boyfriend," said Ed K.

"He'll kick your ass."

"More."

"He'll really kick your ass."

"Is he tall, short, thin, fat? Is he gay? Does he have a temper? Does he get you in a headlock and never let go."

"He's tall. He's built well."

"Good. What does he do for a living."

"He's a photographer," she said.

The music sped up. The music said *get the hell off this road*. The music said that the church was waiting and even if Ed K. never gave it honest respect, it wanted him. Patient churches eat impatient students. Hurt me.

Mary was sweating under her canvas jacket. Once she stopped arguing, she seemed strangely calm. She didn't know if we were going to kill her, abandon her or rape her. She didn't seem to care.

Ten minutes later, eight miles out of her way, Ed K. told me to stop. Ed K. jumped out, opened her door and ordered her out. She left with her head down and her shoulder bag in her hands.

"Just walk back the way you came," he said very friendly, as if we had just done her a favor. She didn't snivel. She didn't whine. She was walking away.

"If you're lucky someone will give you a ride back."

"Fuck you," she yelled. She didn't mean it. And that's the last we were supposed to hear of Mary Gunderson with the red hair and the canvas bag.

Ed K. changed into his kimono. The church looked like a barn. It could hold four hundred lovers of Christ. Most Sundays, three hundred showed up. I was hoping that he'd preach against the accumulation of useless wealth. Truth? I didn't care. I told Ed K. to go inside without me. I had wanted to go inside but Mary ruined it. I needed to catch up on sleep. Ed K. didn't argue. I had my reasons. He didn't want to hear them.

~

I closed my eyes and I didn't open them for an hour. I woke to the screams and the flames. With my keys in the ignition, I heard that great roar of the world falling on itself. I saw a fat man, a man whose hand had grabbed mine only weeks before. He was running. His face was bleeding and his belly was jiggling; he wasn't jolly.

I thought I saw Mary Gunderson, walking up to the church. Everything was tearing at reality. I knew the angels were looking out for Ed K. as he approached my car. He was still wrapped in his kimono and a beatific half-smile. I said hello and he said hello and that's what you get when you dance the two-step.

Ed K. knocked on the window and began speaking in tongues. I'm not talking about Korean. I'm talking about that charlatan snake-oil tongue—the bidda bidda boop tongue. The didi didi dididi di di HEY tongue sounds so impressive when you are in the room full of the big boppers from the high and mighty; suck on the dark roots. When Jesus is coming to your room and grabs you by your cheap suit, you need to take your head and put it between your legs. When you speak, let the biddy-bopping angels take you by the mouth.

That was Ed K. at my car door, speaking with that wholehearted balderdash, that lip-smacking arrogance. The church was burning and it came from Heaven. Ed K. forgave hipsters, hippies and redheads. I heard the angels in Ed K's voice and I knew. I knew. I knew how it was all going down. The fire had reached the earth and the clouds were opening up to pour blessing upon us all—rain, glory, and fancy dancing.

Hooka hay. Hoka hey. Heyka. Heyka. Yeah.

I know you heard the way demons burned in that church. You heard about their screams and their anguish but you never saw the peace in their eyes. You never heard the demons casting out flames, leaving sinless souls for Jesus. Fifty-two dead. Fifty-two dead in a church on a Sunday morning. Ed K. with his double life and me with my rude flesh, my sinful eyes and my debased hypocrisies. We heard it.

And you know how it is when you're sitting in a bar and you're thinking that you want to go home, but you need one more drink. One more exchange with the personal trainer from down the street even though you know that she doesn't want to fuck you. You heard yourself blow it when you could have said something funny but you went for sincere. Then you tried be funny, and you sounded creepy. You opened up your mouth and the banal shit came marching forth. And you said to yourself, fuck, maybe I can just get this started again, but nothing will work when you're that drunk and stupid.

Ed K. jumped into the passenger seat. "Drive," he said, and I said "Yeah," and I said "Hallelujah," and my foot hit the gas and the road zoomed beneath us. I heard screams echoing past my ears. I put on the music of the saved and soulful, the damned and bitter. I hear you, God. I hear you, Jesus. And Ed K. said, "Don't repeat that shit."

I wanted to stop the car. No silence. No peace. No love. Hear you maidens of Israel. Hear this and weep. Your breasts are bouncing gazelles, but one day they'll be paper bags. That's your world, unless you fall in the pits. Fall in the shit. Fall into salvation. Hallelujah.

Ed K. laughed holy fire. Ed K. hummed. And Ed K. sang. I just drove, hoping for instructions. Hear me and make me your slave, Lord. Again I shouted hallelujah.

The clouds took the sky and the wind tortured the chrome. The trees broke. Dead rabbits fell to that lonely pavement. I heard a trumpet; only one trumpet. The angel of death was busy. And then I heard it again. I heard the words of my intoxicated father. Words that made me suspect that life wasn't right. Dad always told me that I had a nice ass. He'd take out a ruler and I wondered if I measured up. He never touched me. I wanted Jesus to whisk me away from sin. I wanted Jesus to steal my sins, my memories, my pain, my degradation. The sky was breaking.

And there she was again, walking down the road. Walking toward us, her jean jacket muddy and her red hair out for all the world to see. Her lips formed in a smile.

"Keep driving," said Ed K., but he was not my master. Nor was I. I heard my voice say something unkind. I wanted to break my own windows. I wanted to buy forgiveness with thirty cloves of silver.

"Hello," she said, leaning into the car. She looked taller. The rains came, splattering everything in a hazy deluge. She didn't try to get inside; she just leaned in and looked at us. Her eyes were mean but she didn't loose the words sulking on her lips.

"Would you like a ride?" I said. Ed K's face got tight. I heard my voice again ask the question. The question stalked the air.

She took the back door handle and crawled inside. I drove back to the church. She didn't speak. She knew that she was in good company. The Jesus radio sang loud. The road beckoned us dark and wet. Some days I talk to trees. Some days I talk to Jesus.

"Stop here," she said when we were back at the church. The fire trucks blocked our path. Ed K. trembled. She released her body from the backseat and walked to the fire. Her dress was clinging to her legs.

"Should we go?" I said.

"No," said Ed K.

I almost turned the key to spite him. I watched her walk to a fire truck and tear her denim jacket from her arms. She was wearing a black bra under her thin dress. I didn't hear Ed K. crying. She tore her clothes as she walked to the ambulance. She screamed and cried in perfect deception.

I watched her act. I saw her deception. And then the cops dragged Ed K. from my passenger seat; I heard the crime dockets. I didn't believe in anything but Jesus and the road.

Mary Gunderson is a state's witness. I don't know what she thinks she saw when she was on the road walking away. She definitely wasn't inside the church. She wouldn't have been alive if she was inside. Mary Gunderson was in my rearview mirror. I did not drive her all the way to church. Ed K. did not invite her inside. She did not see Ed K. light a lamp and throw it into the flowers. She did not see him light all the Easter decorations at once. She did not hear him order the congregation to stay, sit, and burn in purification. She couldn't have seen a bemused look on his face as his brethren held her down and tried to save her from sin. She's lying. The whole story is bullshit.

The sefirot keep bopping. I no longer listen to country music or gospel. I listen to jazz and I hear the Lord coming through the silences. Slap. Pop. Bang. God's fucking with you.

**Tim Lieder** has been published in publications like *Everyday Fiction* and *Silverthought,* but this is his first pro-rate sale. In 1995, he accidentally founded **Dybbuk Press** by editing a short story collection and losing the original publisher. Recently, he edited *She Nailed a Stake Through His Head: Tales of Biblical Terror,* a multi-author horror anthology where all of the horror stories are based on Bible stories.

His blog is at **marlowe1.livejournal.com.**

# THE MEAT FOREST

by John Haggerty

The shot-callers had been fighting over the fresh meat for half an hour when Dmitri showed up. The new kid was covered in mud, the thin drizzle doing nothing to clean him off, but it was clear he was a prime cut. He was tall and good-looking, with the sort of smooth, clear skin and big slabs of muscle that you can only get if you have a lot of time on your hands. He was obviously an owner, but they dropped him just like they had the rest of us—laid down some tear gas, gyroed in, and then kicked him out into the rain and stinking mud without even touching down. When the yard boys got a look at him and word spread, the shot-callers were there in a flash, swarming him like sharks, looking for their piece.

A circle had formed, and everyone was gathered around, jeering, making lewd suggestions, showing their hardest faces while the big boys argued. The kid just stood there. He looked paralyzed, as though he couldn't believe how bad his life had gotten, and how quickly. I watched him from the edge of the crowd. He was probably in his early twenties, but his face was soft like a child's, as if nothing had ever been demanded of him. Surrounded by the mob of shouting, emaciated men, I imagine he had never felt so alone and lost and afraid in his life.

Nobody was backing down and it looked certain that there was going to be a beef. And then Dmitri arrived—just walked right into the middle of everything—and that was enough to shut all of those *chainiks* up. Suddenly, there was complete silence, everybody standing nervously around, waiting to see what would happen next. Dmitri circled around the boy a couple of times, a thin smile on his face. The kid stood rigid and still, even when Dmitri playfully slapped him across the buttocks. After a few moments, he turned to the shot-callers. "Nobody touches him. He's mine."

"Bullshit." It was Oleg, head of the New Odessa crew. He was big and ambitious, trying to make a name for himself. "My boys saw him first. He belongs to us." He looked around at his men with a big smile. "You can have him when we're done with him. If there's anything left." A soft, mean chuckle spread through the crowd.

Dmitri's skin flared a dull red, his bioluminescent implants responding to his anger. He stepped up to Oleg, who flinched in spite of himself. "I said he's mine," he whispered, the thin sibilance of his voice somehow carrying to the edge of the crowd. "One more word and the forest will have you."

The two stared at each other for a long moment, and then Oleg looked away. "Fine. Take him," he spat. "What would we do with a soft little bitch like that anyway?" He smiled around at his crew, but none of them would meet his gaze.

Dmitri gave a laugh. "Follow me, boy," he said, and the kid trailed after him through the parting mob.

Nobody fucked with Dmitri. When they dropped him, some guys walked off, right into the forest, just to get away from him. He was connected, but that wasn't really the whole story. Rumors followed him around, shit horrible enough to make even the old camp lifers, guys who had seen mankind at its very worst, shake their heads in shock. He was thin—almost to the point of emaciation—like all of the rest of us, but everything else set him apart. Prison tattoos and ritual scars covered him from the top of his shaved head down to his feet. He was nearly black with them, elaborate, gothic designs that the experienced could read like a book—robberies, murders, mob allegiances made and broken—the whole history of his criminal life painted on his flesh. He had rows of bioluminescent implants embedded in ridges from the top of his head and down his arms, legs and torso, and they flashed away underneath the tattoos, like lamps through smoke. And when he looked at you, it was like he was looking at some kind of farm animal, like you were a carcass hanging on a hook and he was idly wondering how much you would fetch per pound.

~

Dmitri approached me a few days later. I was sitting at the perimeter, staring through the mist toward the edge of the forest. I went there a lot, killing time right at the camp boundary where you could feel the hum of the electrodes. There were no fences, just the fear of the forest to keep us in, and the electric field to keep it out.

When I first got to the camp, and the hunger really started getting a grip on me, I dreamt only of food, of long tables piled meters deep in greasy red meat. Then I began dreaming of the hunger itself, of dying slowly of a desperate dissatisfaction, of never having enough. Lately, though, I had started dreaming of the forest, and I didn't like to think about what that meant.

"You spend a lot of time out here," he said softly. I hadn't heard him come up behind me, and I started when he spoke.

"I've been watching you. You're out here all the time, looking at the forest. In the camps, that means one of two things. Either you want out, or you're about to give yourself to it. Which is it with you?"

"You shouldn't be talking to me." I was a political prisoner, at the very bottom of the prison hierarchy. Dmitri was breaking one of the great camp taboos, associating with a lower caste member like myself.

Dmitri laughed in my face. "Who is going to stop me? I do what I want." He looked out into the drizzly evening. "I can get you out of here. Do you want to go?"

"What? Out of the camp? How?"

"How do you think?" He nodded toward the gray forest that crowded the perimeter, where the electrodes got too weak to keep it out. "Through that."

"Through the forest? I thought it was impossible."

Dmitri tilted his head up. Beneath his jaw were tattoos of two men's heads, done with red and black ink. Their faces were contorted in an expression of horror;

their eyes closed. He pointed to them. "Do you know what they mean?" he asked. I shook my head. "I've gotten through it twice. The only man in New Russia. I'll take you." He paused, looking me up and down. "It's probably a lost cause. I don't think you'll make it. But if you're interested, come to my hut tonight."

I looked back out at the forest. It wavered in and out of focus in the rain, gray and silent. When I turned back around, Dmitri was already gone.

~

I wandered aimlessly around the edge of the camp until nightfall, my mind restless. The forest had a horrifying reputation. Just the idea of it was enough to keep all of these hard men starving here in the mud and squalor. But life in the camp, especially for a political prisoner, was hard. Over the years a number of my friends had been sent to the camps, and none of them had come back. I didn't want to die here, slowly starving in the constant drizzle and the stinking filth.

I made my way to Dmitri's hut. The boy was waiting for me outside. He pushed me through the vinyl curtain that made up the doorway and followed me in. The place was palatial by camp standards—a patchwork of corrugated metal and plastic sheeting, big enough for three or four men to lie down comfortably. Some fragments of packing crates burned in the corner, giving off a choking black smoke and a little bit of warmth. Dmitri was sitting against the wall near the fire, his skin pulsing idly green.

"Ah, my political," he said jovially as I entered. He held out a bottle. "The camp's finest. Drink."

The murky liquid inside smelled sour and chemical. It was excruciatingly hot going down my throat, and it hit my prison-starved stomach like a fist.

The boy took the bottle from me and sat down next to Dmitri. "So," Dmitri continued, "you're interested in leaving after all."

"I might be. But why me? I'm just a political."

"A political with powerful friends. Friends who apparently miss you very much. Getting you out would be worth a lot of money to me." He leaned forward and passed me the bottle. It was no better the second time.

"How do I know this isn't some kind of setup?"

"Your friend Andrei told me to tell you that if you didn't have a talent for politics, you would be sucking some owner's perfumed cock right now."

I nodded. It was an old joke between me and Andrei.

"And that Nadja isn't going to wait forever."

"Bastard," I muttered under my breath. "Who is going?"

"You, me, and the boy."

"And what about…" I paused.

"The cow? You can say it."

"What about the cow?" I asked. Everyone had heard the stories.

"Hey, boy!" Dmitri nudged him. "Boy, tell him what I taught you."

"Come on, Dmitri," he said. I looked closely at him for the first time since he was dropped. He seemed to be recovering from the initial camp shock—there was a flicker of life in his eyes. But he still looked young and vulnerable, like some sort of baby animal.

Dmitri leaned toward him and hissed, "Tell him, just like I taught you."

The boy shifted a little. Nobody ever felt comfortable being too close to Dmitri. "If you don't know who the cow is, you're the cow," he said.

Dmitri laughed, a dry, dead sound. "Very good. And who is the cow?"

He gave Dmitri a sullen look. "I guess I am."

Dmitri clapped his hands. "Excellent." He turned to me. "You see? He knows his place. And you two will have a lot to talk about in the forest. He's political, too."

I looked at him incredulously. "Him? Political? He's an owner."

"Was an owner," he corrected me. "These idiot children of privilege. You know what he did? He got caught fucking a boyar's wife."

"That makes him stupid, not political."

"It was love," the boy said defiantly.

"You see?" said Dmitri with a smirk. "Love."

"She was married to him, but she didn't love him."

"Tell him the whole story, boy. Tell him how you got caught."

"I told him. Gregor. Her husband. I told him." It came out in a low mumble.

Dmitri took a drink and laughed uproariously. "You see? He walked into the drawing room of a boyar and said 'I am the stupid boy who has been fucking your wife, and I would like a walk in the meat forest.'"

"I told him that I loved Ilse, and that she loved me. And that an honorable man would let her go." There was a note of stubbornness in the boy's voice.

He reached over and pinched the boy's cheek. "Isn't he wonderful, political? Perfect, really. Meat like a cow, brain like a cow."

"Leave him alone, Dmitri." I was shocked to hear my own voice.

Suddenly, Dmitri was on top of me, his hand around my throat. His skin glowed an angry red under the tattoos. His face was inches from mine. I couldn't believe how quickly he had moved. "What did you say to me?"

"Leave him alone." I could feel my throat vibrate under his hand. "He hasn't done anything wrong. He doesn't deserve your bullshit."

Dmitri's breath was hot and bitter. The bioluminescent nodes rippling under his skin gave his face a dull, red illumination, making empty sockets out of his eyes. He pushed me away roughly, banging my head against the metal wall of the hut. "Idealists," he spat, sitting back down. "God save me from idealists. You would even save this empty, useless little boy here? An owner? An idle parasite on your saintly workers?"

"He can't help how he was born. He doesn't know better. He could be reeducated."

"Yes!" Dmitri clapped. "Reeducated. Maybe in a camp just like this?" He leaned forward. "I know you, political. You think you are so superior. So much better than me. A hero to us all. Fighting for truth and justice. But you are no different. You know what the exiles say? Everything eats: the forest, the prisoners, the exiles, the workers, the owners, the gangsters. Even you, political. Everybody, everything in the world is clawing, scratching, killing, eating. Don't fool yourself into thinking you're special."

"No. We're different. I've never…"

"Killed anyone? I have. Many times. It's not such a big deal. No problem at all, really. You'll find this out, too. We're the same. I kill for money, you kill for ideas—or you will very soon. Does that make you so much more special?" He leaned back against the wall, his anger already forgotten, his skin pulsing a cool blue. He closed his eyes. Tattooed on his eyelids were two grinning skulls. "You make me tired. Leave me alone. Both of you." I stood up to leave, and he opened his eyes and looked at me with his impassive butcher's gaze. "There's a food drop tomorrow. We'll get our supplies from that, and then we start walking. Meet me at the drop site at dawn. And get some rest. Tomorrow will be the worst day of your life."

Back outside, in the darkness of the night, the unceasing drizzle felt slimy on my skin, as if blood was falling out of the sky instead of rain.

~

Dmitri and the boy were already at the edge of the drop zone when I got there. Men stood around, puffing up their chests and trying to look fierce. I had never been this close to a resupply before, and it made me nervous.

The three of us stood in silence, waiting. As the dim light of a camp dawn began to grow, the place started to buzz with a cold, prickly feeling of anticipation, equal parts fear, aggression, and animal need. Dmitri cocked his head, and then I heard it, too: the growing whine of the approaching gyros. "It would be best if you stayed well to the side," Dmitri said with a smile.

Suddenly, five great crates plunged out of the sky, breaking open on impact. Supplies spilled out into the mud, and with a roar, everyone charged toward them. The drop zone was instantly in a state of riot as the men scrabbled around for boxes of rations. The prisoners batted at each other with sticks, or clawed and bit and scratched like animals. Anyone who picked up a ration package would be instantly set upon by two or three other men, and beaten until he dropped the food. Then another man would pick it up and the cycle would continue. Dmitri plunged into the chaos like a man swimming in a rough sea, punching and kicking men out of his way, pausing every once in a while to examine the contents of a box. Finally, he stooped, picked something out of the mud and walked back toward me and the boy, stopping a few more times to pick up cartons of food. Near the edge of the riot, a man ran up to Dmitri and tried to pull the food away from him. Dmitri, with only one arm free, gave him a vicious blow to the throat. The man fell to the ground and lay still.

When Dmitri got back to us, he tossed us each a box of rations. It was a vast fortune. Extravagant wealth. More food than I had seen in one place since they had delivered me to this place. "Eat this now," he said. "You will need it. And you, too." He nodded to the boy. "We have to keep all of that luxurious meat on your bones."

I ripped open one of the boxes and started stuffing the food into my mouth. My hands trembled as they tore at the food. I couldn't eat it fast enough.

Dmitri watched with amusement. "Don't you want to see what else I got?" he asked. From under his shirt he pulled out a metal canister with a brass pipe attached to one end. He looked at it admiringly. "They used to call these blowtorches. It's a real antique." He gave us a thin smile. "Blowtorches are very nice to have in the meat forest."

He turned and walked toward the edge of camp. The boy and I followed a few meters behind him.

"Thank you for sticking up for me last night," the boy whispered to me as we walked.

I nodded and looked away. "It's the only nice thing anybody's done for me here. Dmitri's wrong. You are different." His earnest sincerity was almost painful. "And you know, Dmitri's got a temper, but he's all right, really."

"He is not all right." I snapped. "He is…" I stopped as we reached the camp perimeter, where Dmitri stood waiting.

"Okay, children. From now on we live by forest rules," Dmitri said. "Once we get into the forest, we have to be constantly on the move. Keep walking. We can't stop, even for a moment, until we reach an exile clearing. Don't touch anything with your bare skin. The moss is the worst, but everything is dangerous. It can get through clothing in thirty seconds or less. With bare skin, it's faster."

"Exiles. Do they really exist?" I asked.

"Oh, yes. Traveling with them is the only way to get out of the forest. They know how to deal with it. But they're a very touchy people. They need to be handled carefully."

"And how long to the nearest clearing?"

"It's impossible to predict. One day. Two days. Never. It's not easy. If you don't think you can walk for a day and a half straight, you'll probably die out there. Do you still want to go?"

I looked back through the mist at the camp. Sheets of rain hid much of the squalor, but every once in a while the wind would blow the smells our way—garbage, shit, blood. "Let's go," I said, and we stepped across the invisible line marking the maximum amplitude of the electric field.

~

The forest was as gray as it looked from the camp—gray and completely silent. Great coniferous trees stretched upward. The forest floor was marshy and soft, and we slipped constantly in the mud. There was downed timber everywhere, and Dmitri led us on a circuitous line through the maze of fallen trees. This went on, monotonously, for hours, and we started to get careless. The boy was the worst, used to the easy life in the city. He began to trip and fall onto the forest floor, sometimes lying there for a few seconds until Dmitri would kick him to his feet with a few curses.

"You can't stay still, not even for a few seconds. It's everywhere, even if you can't see it." Dmitri would give the boy a push, and we would move on again in silence.

Every once in a while we would happen on a corpse. Still dressed in rotting prison clothing, standing or sitting where the forest got him. When we came on the first one, the boy stood stock still. "Jesus," he whispered.

I looked into the thing's face. It was sickeningly lifelike, a raw, red facsimile of the man it used to be, as if his skin had been flayed from him where he sat—a sculpture of a man carved out of raw meat. As I looked, it seemed to pulsate and move. Dmitri pulled us away. "This one is still pretty active. Not very old. Maybe you knew him. The new ones are the most dangerous. They wake up faster."

"People talk about it, but it never seemed real until now." The boy was pale and shaken.

"The glory of the meat forest," Dmitri exclaimed as we walked on. "A massive fungal mat. Millions of square miles. It underlies all of the taiga. That's why it's such a wonderful place for the owners to put all of their prison camps. It eats everything it touches."

"It's horrible," I said.

"So judgmental, political. It is merely following its nature. As do I, and you, and yes, as does our beloved cow."

~

Toward midday, Dmitri allowed us to pause for food. "Keep your feet moving," he said. "Touch nothing."

We started eating, walking in place, trying to keep from touching anything for too long.

"I almost killed you last night, political." Dmitri said as we ate. "It was the businessman in me that spared your life." He laughed. "You see, I have values, too."

"That's not a value. It's greed."

"Oh, what's the difference? We each have our guiding principles." After a pause, he said, "You know, if we make it out of here, we should keep in touch. I know what you politicals are like. You're so noble and pure at the beginning. But then reality gets in the way. You start to cut corners, make compromises. That's when you will need someone like me. I think we will come to value one another greatly. Men like you are very good for business."

"I don't want anything from you, Dmitri."

He gave me his mirthless smile. "You wanted out of the camp. Your first compromise. The first of many. But enough. Let's get moving."

As the day wore on, the constant movement began to wear on me. My legs ached with a dull pain, their movements sluggish. It was as if they were no longer legs at all, but rusty pieces of machinery. The boy was worse, not walking as much as falling forward with each step, stabbing a stiff leg out at the last minute to prevent himself from pitching headlong to the forest floor.

I thought about stopping, closing my eyes and lying down, letting the forest take me. Each time these thoughts arose, I would push them away, trying to give myself reasons to keep walking. I thought again of food, of great, hot mouthfuls of meat. I thought of my friend Andrei, his cynical humor hiding an almost painful sincerity. I thought of Nadja, her pale northern skin and her sly smile, how she sat silent and angry through my trial, indifferent to the danger. And I thought of my father, the arguments he would have with my mother. "The powerful will always prey on the weak. It will never change," she would say, her pretty face flushed. "You endanger all of us, and in the end it will make no difference."

He would smile at her gently. "Yes, but if I see injustice and let it stand, then the injustice infects me. I can't stop. Please understand." They came for him when I was 16, and after that my mother refused to speak his name, afraid that they were still watching, listening, that they would come for the rest of us, too.

"Shit. Where is the boy?" Dmitri's voice broke into my daze.

I turned in a quick circle. He was twenty feet behind us, leaning against a tree. "Shit. Shit." Dmitri ran toward him, pulling out the blowtorch. He dragged the boy upright, and it was as if his shoulder had become plastic, with red, meaty strands stretching from the trunk to his arm. "Hold him steady!" The boy's head lolled on his shoulders. His half-open eyes were dim and glazed. Dmitri lit the torch and held the flame to the red membranes connecting the boy to the tree. They blackened and parted under the heat, but kept whipping around like tentacles, searching for their host. On the boy's shoulder was a raw wound, filled with dozens of red, squirming worms. Dmitri held the blowtorch to his flesh. There was a stench of burning meat. The boy jerked a bit but made no sound.

Dmitri took hold of the boy's damaged arm. "We have to move faster now. It becomes more active when it has fed." We started moving again, half running, half dragging the boy through the gray trees.

We were both puffing with the exertion. I heard rustling noises behind us, the first sounds since we started walking. I looked back, and the forest behind us was suddenly, twitchingly alive. Clumps of moss squirmed on the ground and the downed timber, as if the whole forest was flexing its muscles.

"Faster," Dmitri said. Around us, red tendrils began to protrude from the mossy trees and ground. "Don't let them touch your skin."

"How far do we have to go like this?"

"Now that it's awake, it will keep looking for us. We can't stop."

"What about the boy? What's wrong with him?"

"The fungus carries a substance that acts like a sedative. He'll be useless for at least thirty minutes. Until he comes to, we have to carry him." The forest was squirming now, with meaty tentacles blindly searching for prey.

We were growing tired, and our movements slowed. We lurched drunkenly about as the boy's weight shifted between us. Behind us the forest was a snarl of fungus, spun with a huge spider web of meat. The air had begun to fill with a noxious smell, half flowery perfume, half rotten meat.

"Look," Dmitri said. "Over there."

Off to the left, there was a faint brightness, a break in the undifferentiated mist. Cold, slimy appendages dropped from above, brushing at my neck and hair. I hunched my shoulders against them and tried to walk faster.

Suddenly, we emerged into a large open clearing. I felt the familiar hum of an electromagnetic field. At first I thought we had come in a great circle, walked back into the camp, but then I saw the exiles. There were perhaps a dozen—men, women, and a few children—gathered around a smoky fire. They were thin and hard, and they looked at us with a disturbing intensity. After a long moment, a man stepped forward to greet us.

"Everything eats," he said.

"Everything eats," Dmitri replied.

"Everything eats, everything eats, everything eats," the tribe behind him chanted in unison. They were stooped, emaciated and pale. Their skin was pitted and furrowed with scars. They surrounded the boy, poking at his gym muscles, whispering to themselves.

"We come out of the forest in need of help," Dmitri said.

"You have awakened it," the tribesman replied. "We will not be able to move for days." Dmitri stayed silent. The man looked around the clearing, and into the rustling forest. "There is not much food, and everything eats. The laws of the forest cannot be broken. You may stay with us, but you must give us something in return. What do you have for us?"

"A cow," Dmitri said. "We have brought you a cow."

"And where is the cow?" the tribesman asked.

Dmitri paused, and then pointed at me. "He will tell you."

There was a long silence. I could hear the ravenous whisper of the forest behind me, a vast wasteland of primordial hunger, all that need, just under the skin. I looked at the boy. In his stupor, he again looked like a child.

"I can't," I said. Dmitri moved over to me.

"Choose carefully," he whispered. "Your people need you. Nadja needs you. The revolution cannot continue without you. The boy is an owner. A parasite. There are millions like him, sucking at the life of the workers. It is such a small sacrifice." He pushed me toward the exile leader. "Go on. Tell him."

I looked out at the twitching forest, at the sickly tribe, up at the sky. I closed my eyes against the rain. "The boy," I said, into the hungry silence. "The boy is the cow."

The tribesman nodded. "Excellent. He is a good cow. Everything eats."

"Everything eats," Dmitri and I responded in unison.

**John Haggerty** is a former software engineer and a volunteer prison teacher living in the San Francisco Bay Area. His work has appeared or is forthcoming in *Confrontation, The MacGuffin, Opium Magazine, Santa Monica Review, Vestal Review* and *War, Literature & the Arts,* among others. His work was a runner-up for the 2007 Bridport Prize and received Pushcart nomination. He is currently working on his first novel.

# Tying Notes to Bricks
## A CONVERSATION WITH D. HARLAN WILSON

by John Boden

D. Harlan Wilson is a tour de force in the "Bizarro" movement. Intelligent and hilarious and disturbing would be the first three words I would use to describe his work...barring the descriptive expletives, that is. The best thing about a D. Harlan story is that you literally have no idea where it will take you; each paragraph is its own unique animal, sometimes feral and snarling, other times tame and lethargic. I was fortunate enough to get to know D a little after reviewing his fantastic novella, *"Peckinpah."* We emailed and chatted a bit and he granted me an interview. So being careful to avoid making sudden movements, I give you D. Harlan Wilson.

~

**JB: Tell us a little bit about how you became the man you are now. What turned you into the twisted wordsmith we know today?**

**DHW:** Protein, anabolic steroids, elementary school brawls, Steve Perry, cheap scotch, collecting throwing stars, dreams of Idaho, and Rambo movies made me the man I am today. I don't do those things anymore, though. Which is to say, I do them in moderation. Sometimes.

I didn't get into writing fiction until graduate school when I started working on my M.A. degree in the critical study of English at UMass-Boston. That was in 1995. I partied my way through my B.A. at Wittenberg University in Fratboyland, but I majored in English, and I wrote bad poetry. At UMass, I took a fiction writing class for fun, and I was hooked. I didn't get anything published until, I think, 1999. I probably shouldn't have had much published until recently. I'm almost 40 and just now beginning to feel comfortable as an author.

Nice of you to call me a wordsmith. I've always been more interested in language than story, which shows in my work, for better and for worse. But I'm very keen on the notion that our identities and selfhoods are constructed by language. It's what makes us human, and that's a story in itself. Continually developing my lexicon, and refining my ability to craft syntax, has been very important to me in adult life. That's a big reason why I write what I write. Not that stories aren't told, of course.

**JB: My introduction to you and your work came through my purchase of *The Bizarro Starter Kit* books...and I thought, "Wow, these cats are out there." I particularly liked your story "Cops & Bodybuilders" for its sheer ridiculousness. There is so much humor in your work, almost Pythonesque humor, that you either love and get or don't and don't. How did you get there?**

**How did you end up where you currently reside on the radar of Bizzaro and surrealist fiction?**

**DHW:** Thanks for the kind words, Johnny. I agree: readers generally either love or hate my writing. Or they just say it's weird and leave it at that. Some of that has to do with humor being so subjective. For the most part it's a result of how I estrange readers by destabilizing their expectations. My upcoming fiction collection, *They Had Goat Heads,* has received a few preliminary reviews with varying degrees of praise and skepticism, although they're mostly positive. One review was quite scathing. Here's an excerpt:

"It's extremely rare that I genuinely dislike a piece of fiction. So why did I dislike *They Had Goat Heads?* I think the answer lies in the definition of fiction. Plot. Characters. All that jazz. In these short stories, the elements of fiction are barely discernible. The moment some semblance of plot begins to pop up, it's killed instantly by a random slew of profanity or nonsense. This weird hybrid between bad poetry and schizophrenic prose is 'repetitive, endless torture' to sit through. Don't waste your money."

So, yeah, uh, this reviewer didn't like the book. And it makes sense given what the reviewer clearly looks for in fiction. That's fair. And to be expected, on occasion. But why does all fiction have to do the same old shit? Fuck that, seriously. I make a concerted effort to subvert normative conventions. If you want convention, go read one of a trillion other plot-oriented, character-driven books out there. I try to do new and different things, sometimes successfully, sometimes not. I've always written stuff that falls rather far off the beaten path. I recall being heavily influenced by William S. Burroughs (e.g., *Naked Lunch* and the cut-up trilogy) when I first started writing. Like a lot of would-be "avant-garde" authors. Not so much for his subject matter as for the dynamism and innovative nature of his prose. Kafka really resonated with me, too. Anyway, it was years before I began writing publishable stories, and over time I developed my own style and voice. And my style and voice continue to evolve, like any writer that sticks with it.

In addition to Bizzaro, my writing has fallen into multiple genres and subgenres, including science fiction, fantasy, horror, splatterpunk, splattershtick (my favorite), irrealism, postmodernism, absurdism, critifiction, "literary" fiction, interstitial fiction, etc. It's all of these things. And none of them.

*[Note: See the Strange Goods and Other Oddities section on page 55 for a review of They Had Goat Heads.]*

**JB: How do you see the genre of Bizzaro and where do you see it in the brickwork of the fiction genres? I realize it is a fairly young genre, but not a young style...there have been writers and works all throughout the history of written word that have been hard—or impossible—to categorize.**

**DHW:** Like I always say, Bizarro is a marketing tool conceived of and disseminated by a cadre of small press publishers to sell books. It's proved to be an effective marketing tool. But, as you infer, there have been lots of weird and offbeat writing movements in the past—some of which (e.g., Surrealism) were devised for the same purposes.

Bizarro is a subgenre of speculative fiction, I suppose. Mainly it's distinguished by cartoon absurdism, grotesque playfulness, and cult (film) aesthetics. Some of my writing has certainly exhibited these features. But the core Bizarro writers have a much more refined idea about what it should be. They don't like narrative experimentalism, for instance, which I do a lot of. And they tend to shy away from "literary" fiction. Most of my fiction these days is literary (i.e., metafictional and allusive); it's more adequately labeled critifiction, combining fiction with critical theory. The point is, there are different kinds of Bizarro fiction. The kind I write has been called irrealism. This is arguably a subgenre of speculative fiction in and of itself, but whatever. Bizarro has gained momentum and wider recognition since its inception. I think it's approaching stasis at this point. But milk it while it lasts, right?

**JB: Tell us about the journals you work with—*Extrapolation* and *The Dream People*—as well as what projects are on your horizon.**

**DHW:** *They Had Goat Heads* will be published officially at the end of September 2010 by Atlatl Press. Then, in January 2011, I have a novel coming out through Raw Dog Screaming Press, *Codename Prague,* the second installment in my "scikungfi" trilogy. The first novel in the trilogy was *Dr. Identity, or, Farewell to Plaquedemia,* published back in 2007. The third and final installment, *The Kyoto Man,* will come out in 2012 or 2013; I've completed a first draft but it needs considerable revision, per usual. I'm also working on a series of interconnected novelettes, together called *Curd,* each of which features the same protagonist in different near-future contexts and narrative lifescapes. Not sure when that will be finished. As for criticism, I'm halfway through a short book on John Carpenter's film *They Live* for UK publisher Wallflower Press cultographies series. That's slated to be released in 2012.

I've been the editor-in-chief of *The Dream People: A Journal of Irreal Texts* (www.dreampeople.org) since 2006. It's an online journal put out biannually. We publish short fiction, novel excerpts, book reviews, microcriticism, interviews (sometimes), comics (sometimes), and artwork. I've only just taken on the role of reviews editor for *Extrapolation,* the oldest academic journal of science fiction criticism in America. It's tedious, but fun, and very rewarding. Basically I gather new books of science fiction criticism from publishers, assign them to reviewers, and edit the reviews. I'm really happy to be part of *Extrapolation's* team; they're a sharp bunch of editors and scholars.

**JB: What are your thoughts on the current state of the small press, the POD places and the antho mills? Do you feel it is on the way out, as many claim,**

or just changing and evolving to remain viable in the current age of Kindle and e-books?

**DHW:** POD and e-books will take over. Soon. They already are. Consider the fall of Leisure Books' horror imprint recently; instead of mass market paperbacks, they're moving to PODs and e-books because they're so much cheaper and easier to produce. Bigger publishers will hang on for awhile. But POD printing presses have the capacity to manufacture books that in many cases look (and *are*) much better than, say, books put out by HarperCollins, Random House, etc. Print books won't disappear—people still like to hold them in their hands and turn the pages. I certainly do. But e-readers constitute an exploding market. Some critics think print books and e-books can't co-exist; it must be one or the other. That's silly. There's room (and consumer demand) for all of it.

**JB: What and who do you like to read?**

**DHW:** My favorite author is Steve Aylett. His novels and stories strike chords with me more than any other author I've read, dead or alive. They're funny, clever and satirical, and they make me think critically and creatively; I always learn something, either about the world and the human condition or about writing itself. That's what I aspire for in my own work. Sounds like a simple combination, but it's very difficult to do effectively. Consummate Aylett books include *Slaughtermatic* (novel), *The Inflatable Volunteer* (novel), *Toxicology* (stories), *LINT* (pseudobiography) and *The Caterer* (comic). But everything's good. Check out his library at www.steveaylett.com.

Honestly I don't like most of the fiction I read. I'm an elitist, admittedly, and selective to a fault—at least if I'm reading for pleasure. Many of the books I read are for the courses I teach or for literary criticism and reviews I'm writing. Right now I'm rereading Richard Wright's *Native Son* and Ralph Ellison's *Invisible Man* for a course I'm teaching on African-American literature this Fall. Both are loooooong books, doorstoppers, and I like them, but more for their historical context, although each author demonstrates a certain linguistic prowess and pace, and that means a lot to me.

Primarily I read speculative fiction, though—science fiction, steampunk, (post)cyberpunk, splatterpunk, etc. In this area, Philip K. Dick is my touchstone. That guy was an idea factory and produced hundreds of stories and novels throughout his career. And he does a fine job mingling humor with more serious sociocultural issues and themes.

Fiction aside, I'm an avid reader of literary theory, history, and criticism. Especially the latter. I subscribe to a bunch of science fiction academic journals and always try to keep up with critical trends in the field.

**JB: What trips your trigger as far as non-writing time...hobbies?**

**DHW:** I don't have a lot of hobbies, unless watching movies and TV counts. I guess my biggest hobby is lifting weights. I'm into bodybuilding, always revising and refining my diet, and probably overtraining: lately I've been working out 60-90 minutes 5-6 days a week. Some of that time is spent doing cardio (treadmill, elliptical, etc.), but mostly it's pumping iron. I do it as much for my health and image as I do for my psyche. I'm a high-strung fella, generally speaking, and I need that daily flood of endorphins to keep me on the level.

**JB: Does music play any type of role in the creative process for you? If so, what sort of things do you listen to?**

**DHW:** Yes, music plays a big role. In the past I've gotten many ideas for stories and books from songs. My novel, *Blankety Blank: A Memoir of Vulgaria* (Raw Dog Screaming Press 2008), for instance, sprung like a fountainhead from The Vogue's "Five O'Clock World," a single released in 1965 that, for me, is this deeply eerie yet happy-go-lucky song about capitalism, blip culture, (sub)urbanity, and the centrality of disavowal in western consciousness. The lyrics are simple enough. But they're inflected by the melody and the haunting intonation of the lead singer's voice. It haunts me, anyway.

I listen to all kinds of stuff. Rap. Bebop. Jazz. Metal. Arena Rock. I'm particularly enamored by 1980s pop and punk since I adolesced in that decade. Honestly, though, I don't know much about contemporary music. There are so many permutations and offshoots. Hundreds. I do know that I don't like Country and Christian Rock. And it doesn't help that these are the dominant forms where I live and work in northern Indiana and Ohio. Above all, I prefer classical music. And elevator music. Muzak. That's what I listen to when I write and read.

**JB: Any kind words for anyone, anything? Soapbox time.**

**DHW:** I always have a lot to say. Too much. Permit me to temper and restrict myself to just a few pieces of advice: [1] Don't do a Ph.D. in English unless you are independently wealthy or enjoy being poor and victimized by the specter of plaquedemia. [2] Stay away from Ohio. [3] If you want to be a writer, read your ass off, learn everything you can about the industry, and manage your expectations. [4] Understand that writing is not writing: it's rewriting. [5] Always forgive people, but never forget a fuckin' asshole. [6] Don't walk around with your mouth half open. [7] Visit me online at **www.dharlanwilson.com**.

Thanks, Johnny!

# DRIFT

## by Amanda C. Davis

The snow is made of bugs," said Caden.

I leaned against the kitchen counter beside my firstborn, the kindergarten king, who was sleepily trying to put peanut-butter crackers into his mouth and mostly missing. He watched the window like he listened to lullabies. The heat of the kitchen turned his cheeks red and made his eyelids droop. My unpredictable angel.

"Who told you that?" I asked.

"I saw it." He put a cracker up to my face and I took a messy bite. "Little white bugs."

I wiped my face on my wrist. I would smell like snack time all day. But so what? At that moment I wanted nothing more than to eat peanut butter in a warm kitchen with a little boy who thought that snow was made of bugs.

"Those are called snowflakes," I said. "Like you made in class. Remember?"

He grew thoughtful. "I did mine wrong," he confessed at last. "Mrs. Feaster hung them all up on the wall anyway. Even Martin's, and he didn't listen to the directions. So his is in half." He flapped his hands to signify two halves of a snowflake forever divided by a kindergartener who couldn't pay attention.

"Did you do it wrong like Martin?"

"No." Tones of scandal and scorn.

"Maybe Mrs. Feaster will let you try again."

"No, we have to make snowmen now."

"Oh, okay, snowmen. That sounds like fun."

I put my arm around his shoulders and he let me, which was no longer a guarantee. The curve of his head burrowed into my side, soft and insistent, an echo of our union before birth. Now there was peanut butter on my shirt and I couldn't care less. The cold outside brought us closer inside. The snow lulled us to love.

"Are snowmen made of bugs?" he said.

I held him tighter. "You tell me."

"I hope not."

He sat still for almost a minute before he squeezed out of my arms and ran away.

~

Mrs. Feaster called the next day, before the three of us were quite finished eating dinner. She had the calm, cheery voice of a teacher of the young, and she kept it up even as she was telling me there had been "an incident in the classroom" and she "thought I should be informed."

"Of course," I said, ducking behind a corner so that, if necessary, I could become furious in private. "What happened?"

"Caden went to the cork board and started drawing on other children's snowflakes," she said. "I spoke with him about only touching his own things, but I thought you might want to reinforce the lesson at home."

I felt embarrassed, partly because I had birthed a vandal, partly because I had tried something similar with paper pilgrim hats when I was five and still remembered the shame. "I'm glad you told me. I'm so sorry—"

"No permanent damage," she said cheerfully. "We flipped them around and they were as good as new. Thanks for your cooperation. Caden's a joy. He's never done anything destructive like this before."

I swore on my honor that he never would again, and returned to the table.

He looked guilty. He knew I knew. "That was Mrs. Feaster," I told my husband Bryant: a roundabout way of telling Caden.

"What did she want?" said Bryant. He directed the question to me but watched our son the graffitist while he said it.

I sprung the trap. "Caden? Do you know why she called me?"

He frowned deeply at the table and whispered, "I got in trouble."

"Oh yeah?" Bryant, like Mrs. Feaster, had the superpower of keeping his voice light and friendly no matter what he was saying. I did not. "For what?"

"For fixing the snowflakes."

Bryant's eyebrows floated higher. "'Fixing' them?"

He nodded. "They did it wrong."

I had to jump in: "You told me only Martin did it wrong."

He wagged his head in a dogged *no*. "Everybody did it wrong. They didn't have any eyes."

They didn't have any *eyes?* Our conversation from the previous afternoon came back to my mind. "Caden told me yesterday that he thought that snowflakes looked like bugs," I said to Bryant, who bit back a laugh. "Is that what you were doing, Caden? Drawing on eyes so they looked more like bugs?"

"Uh-huh."

I wasn't sure what part of his thinking to correct first, so I chose science. "Honey, snowflakes don't have eyes. They just look like bugs because they're small and have little branches that look like legs. Everyone made them just fine." On to the ethics. "You can't draw on other people's snowflakes, even if you think they made them wrong, because they don't belong to you. You can only draw on yours. Nobody else's."

The next day he brought home his snowflake, crayoned on both sides with eyes and antennae and little claws on the end of each branch, and proudly told me he didn't fix anyone else's this time, just his own. I asked whether everyone had brought home their snowflakes. He ran off without answering. I never found out whether the snowflakes had been sent home to make way for snowmen, or whether Mrs. Feaster found his toothed, taloned snow-bug grotesque amid the pure white paper snow.

~

He came in from the Saturday snow as quickly as he had gone out into it. What I could see of his face past the snow suit was red.

"The snow bugs bit me," he said, and burst into tears.

I dropped to my knees. Two stiff little marshmallow-arms tried to hug me; the clammy, snotty face pressed into my neck. I knelt in the melting snow and said *"Shhh"* until my clothes were soaked. "It's okay, it's okay. It's not bugs, honey, you're just cold. Snowflakes are made of ice. Sometimes they hurt." That didn't seem to comfort him, so I went back to *"Shhh."*

When our body temperatures equalized he pulled away. He still had a blush of red across his nose and both cheeks. I took a closer look. What I had taken for chilly skin was a rash of tiny pink bumps, spaced like stars on his face. I extracted him from the snow suit. He had more where his right mitten met his sleeve.

"What were you doing?" I said carefully, expecting to hear about neighborhood pets or winter-stripped bushes.

"I was outside," he said. His lips trembled again. "I said no."

"No what?"

"I don't want to go with them, Mommy."

*I don't want to go with them.*

Fear froze my chest like the wet snow never could. I had been watching through the window. We lived on a quiet street. But had I turned away at the wrong moment? Had someone slipped into our yard just quickly enough to ask of Caden a terrifying favor? How close had we come to the worst day of our lives?

We did not go back outside. The falling snow made a curtain between us and the world.

~

By the time Bryant came home, the tiny bumps on Caden's face had vanished. My fears had not. The twin panaceas of hot chocolate and cartoons calmed him but were less effective on me. Caden wouldn't give me a straight answer about who had asked him to come with them, so I took Bryant aside to explain the situation and then sent in daddy. He returned looking puzzled.

"He said the snow bugs wanted him to come with them."

I slumped. "He came in with some kind of rash on his face," I said. "He thought the snow bugs bit him. Maybe he put the two things together in his mind."

"Maybe," said Bryant. He took off his tie, slung it across a chair. "Look, he's fine. He's here. I'll call a couple of the neighbors, see if anyone saw anything. *Snow bugs,"* he added, with an aren't-we-adults look. "Maybe he made it all up."

"You didn't see him crying," I said. But as the scents of dinner filled the house and Caden's laughter grew in gales under Bryant's watch, I came to believe Caden must have invented the situation—or at least, escalated it from something benign.

He must have.

The alternative was unbearable.

~

Caden refused to go to church.

"Come on, buddy, you love Mr. Ai's class," Bryant said, when Caden announced this at breakfast.

"I am not going," said the apple of my eye.

"Oh, yes you are," I lovingly rejoined.

"No!"

Bryant, the bargainer, said, "Why not?"

"I don't wanna go outside." Petulance slurred his words. "It's snowing."

Bryant and I exchanged a look. "Maybe we could skip once," he said to me, in a soft adult voice meant to bounce past Caden. "In the light of, you know, yesterday."

I shook my head and brought the volume of the conversation back to Caden level. "In this house," I said, "we go to church or we are *carried* to church."

"Just like the cavemen did," said Bryant, with a wink.

"You're not helping," I informed him.

"I don't want to go to church and YOU CAN'T MAKE ME," said Caden, before he wiggled off his chair and ran upstairs with shirttails flying.

He proved to be incorrect on that point. But he shouted "No!" the entire trip, and although he settled down immediately upon being dropped in the vestry, I whispered an apology to Bryant during the sermon. The looks we would have gotten for skipping church were nothing compared to the ones he got for showing up with a screaming child across his shoulder.

~

During the walk home, clusters of bumps appeared on Caden's hands and face. I made Bryant examine them while I made a blitzkrieg search of the Internet. The Internet, according to its ways, turned up everything from Lyme disease to an allergy to water.

("That's not possible," said Bryant. I said, "It is, there's a girl in England," and even when I showed him the news article he insisted it was faked.)

The bumps faded before we decided whether to take Caden to the emergency room or not. He hunched on the sofa with a read-along book and a mask of bitter resignation. My heart went out to him. What a thing it is, to be five years old: to be so small that you can be carried where you do not want to go, to be so tender that snowflakes bite like insects. He had entrusted his fears to his mother and I had dismissed them.

What a betrayal.

I crouched before the sofa so that his feet were level with my face. "Hey," I said. "Why don't we go play outside?"

His eyes grew enormous. "No no no. It's snowing."

"I know," I said, "the snow bugs." That caught his attention. "Snow can be a little scary, can't it? But I bet you and me can make it okay."

"Daddy, too?"

I smiled. "Why don't you go ask him?"

He leapt to the floor and dashed to the kitchen. I followed to listen in, and to insinuate silently that Bryant would say yes if he knew what was good for him. He earned his good-husband badge. While Caden was scrambling to get his snow gear, he slid up to me and said, in that adult undertone, "Are you sure about this? Don't you think something outside might've caused those bumps?"

"Maybe," I said. "But if it happens again we'll know exactly what he got into. We can get him into the car right away. This is bigger than bumps."

He nodded thoughtfully. "Our kid's afraid of snow, and it's only November."

Bless him, he understood. "I have a feeling the rash might be psychosomatic," I said. "And I have a feeling that mom and dad might be able to chase away the snow bugs."

I kissed him for luck. Then Caden stomped in singing "PUT ON YOUR BOOTS, PUT ON YOUR BOOTS" in a bellow, wearing his own boots on his hands, and we began the long, hilarious ritual of suiting up to face the snow. Usually it reminded me of harried NASA scientists packing an eager astronaut into his equipment. Today it felt more like dressing for war.

The snow fell in clumps rather than flakes: chilled manna. Caden clung to our hands. We stood under the porch roof for a moment, sizing things up, warriors evaluating the whites of our enemies' eyes; then Bryant and I nodded at each other, and we stepped as a unified frontline into the snowy yard.

Caden's feet sank into the snow to the ankle. He tightened his hold on us. I watched his face; he seemed to be holding his breath. With great reluctance, he turned his cherubic face up and up until it tilted toward the sky. Clustered snowflakes found his eyelashes, his lips. I held my breath.

My son's snow-frosted lips parted. "They're not biting me." He beamed up at me, radiating relief and joy. "They're not biting me!" He roped his arms around my leg. "Mommy, it's okay!" Then he bounded away in big clumsy giant-steps through the snow.

Bryant and I mirrored each other's open-mouthed bemusement. "It's okay," he repeated, eyebrows scrunched.

I sagged. "It's okay."

A badly-packed snowball glanced off my arm. The culprit put his mittens over his face and giggled insanely. He launched himself to the ground to gather more anti-mother missiles.

I screamed because that's what he wanted, and crouched to make my own snowballs. Bryant got there faster, scooping up ammunition one-handed, and retaliated. Caden shrieked with laughter and tossed out an armful of snow, two-handed, back at him. My boys: fully devoted to mutually assured destruction.

I closed my eyes and let the cold crystals come to rest like butterflies on my upturned face. Everything felt warm. This was wonder. This was joy.

*He's going to smack me in the face with a snowball while I'm not looking, I thought. He'll play a prank on his mom, thoughtless and heartless, and I'll love it—because he loves me so much that he wants to make me laugh, and he knows I love him so much he can get away with it. I'll take a snowball to the face for you, Caden. Or a fist or a bullet. No prerequisites at all.*

The snowball did not come.

Bryant touched my arm; through his glove and my coat I felt only the vague warm pressure. "Honey, did you see—?"

I opened my eyes. "What, see what?"

"See where Caden went."

My stomach began to sink like boots in deep snow, like stones in water. "Isn't he just—" I gestured across the yard. His imprint remained where he had stood: my unpredictable snow angel. Nothing more.

"Caden?" Bryant raised his voice, and deepened it at the same time: an injection of fatherly authority. I followed:

"Caden, come out now."

Silence.

Silence and snow.

"Caden!" Something cluttered my throat—I tried to shout past it, but squeaked instead. "Bryant, follow his tracks."

"There are no tracks." He was grave and detached, all business. I hated him suddenly. *"Caden—?* Look, only ones leading here. Not away."

"Then he went back the same—"

"I'm going around the back," he said. I saw then how white his face had grown, white from brow to chin, with red spots of cold on either cheek. His dark eyes swam deep beneath the white brow. "Stay here."

The snow fell harder. Manna turned to ice. My husband strode through the unbroken snow, leaving a man-sized trail where there was no trail the size of a little boy. I was alone.

I went to the last imprint of my son. "Ca—"

The name dried to a rasp in my mouth. The falling snow blinded me, weighed me down. Every flake stung. I swatted at the air with my bare hand, trying to get them away from my face, but they swarmed down my arm, piling into dunes on my fingers, icy and hard. My hand began to ache.

I stared at the space between my fingers. Tiny bumps rose in the soft wells of skin.

*I don't want to go with them.*

*It's made of bugs.*

"It's made of bugs," I whispered. I stared at my hands. The stinging Braille rash rose before my eyes. "Bryant, it's made of bugs. Bryant, *the snow is made of bugs."* I heard him call back to me, but he sounded very, very far away. The noise and pain increased together. Snowflakes grew fingers, and fingers grew talons, and their pinprick faces leered as they hurled past my eyes. "Bryant, they took him, they took him! It's made of bugs! The snow is made of bugs!"

I could not hear his answer over my screams. I stared into the falling white sky, a soft ceiling crashing down to smother me, and the bugs swirled and laughed and showed their black crayon teeth, and the wind pushed drifts into Caden's tracks until they filled with laughing snow bugs—and vanished.

**Amanda C. Davis** is a Pennsylvania engineer with a green thumb, a growing collection of comic books, and a fondness for terrible horror films. You can find her work in *Triangulation: End of the Rainbow, Necrotic Tissue,* and *Goblin Fruit,* among others.

Learn more about her at **www.amandacdavis.com**.

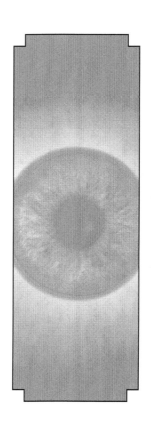

# Worm Central Tonite!

by John Skipp

So I'm burrowing into this dead guy's eyeball, having dispensed with the lid-flap at last. Hard work. Painstaking. Tough to dissolve.

But tasty? Yes.

Worth the effort? Absolutely.

A little perspective is a wonderful thing.

For example:

I'm not a big eater, but I do love to eat. I mean, sure, I shit my own body weight daily. But as graveyard worms go, I am fairly svelte.

Not like Braxis, already plowing straight through the glazed pupil beside me like an animate sausage arrow in relentless bullseye mode. That guy is so fucking fat he can barely undulate without popping his casing, but away he goes, tail flipping past my face, riding the gravy train straight down the optic nerve railroad.

He will beat me to the brain, no question.

He always does.

There's a lot of traffic at Worm Central tonite. Fresh meat. Always a cause for celebration. People haven't been dying fast enough lately. I've got a bad feeling this dustbowl town is drying up.

But here in the socket, pushing through to the goo, things couldn't be more moist and juicy. I could wallow in here all day. I love those moments when I see how they see as a *pure experience,* disconnected from the conclusions they draw one micro-instant later, when the rest of the relays kick in.

But there is no substitute for the Big Picture.

As such, I squirm through, swallowing just enough to show me blue skies in a green world. The last sights they saw, before closing forever.

Then I'm squeezing through the cracks in the bone—somebody definitely took a hammer to this clown—and on my way to the main course.

Most of the worms I know like to soak in muscle memory. What it felt like to have arms. What it felt like to have legs. Some are all about the genitalia, those uncanny vibrations. (I went through that phase.)

Some mystics seek out the heart, in search of love. I tried that, too.

Most head straight for the guts, and what they know. Being none the wiser is fine with them.

Me, I like to know what it was like to grapple with it all. To have ALL those things going on at once. To have words to describe it.

Again: a little perspective is a wonderful thing.

But to each their own. Tonight, we dine. Riddling this otherwise-empty vessel with the only life it will ever know again.

Remembered, one bite at a time.

Tonight, I will learn how this poor bastard lived. How he died. How much

TV he watched. How much he hated his job. How much he got laid. How many people he hurt. How many times he smiled and meant it.

What he thought about his place here on Earth.

Not a bad gig for a worm, all told.

I slither after Braxis, grab my front row seat, take a big bite of cerebral DNA…

*…and the first thing I taste is his fear, the wild synapse-flashes of his meat's impending end. It combines with the eyeball-memory of the swing and connect, a hammer indeed, cracking skull and yanking bone back out, the claw end wet and caked and red…*

Very scary. No doubt about it. In terms of intensity, it beats the fuck out of *Scarface:* a movie this dimwit clearly loved.

But here's the thing. *The end is the end,* every meat-go-round. I will die soon, too. Just another squiggly vessel.

But my memories will pass on. From flesh to flesh to flesh.

No real end.

And no forgetting.

As such, I snuggle into the cranial folds. Chew past the terror-bites, as they gradually give way to deeper, more rewarding bounty.

Just another night in Worm Central.

Forever and ever.

Amen.

**John Skipp** is a *New York Times* bestselling author, editor, zombie godfather, compulsive collaborator, musical pornographer, black-humored optimist and all-around Renaissance mutant. His early novels from the 1980s and 90s pioneered the graphic, subversive, high-energy form known as splatterpunk. His anthology *Book of the Dead* was the beginning of modern post-Romero zombie literature. His work ranges from hardcore horror to whacked-out Bizarro to scathing social satire, all brought together with his trademark cinematic pace and intimate, unflinching, unmistakable voice. From young agitator to hilarious elder statesman, Skipp remains one of genre fiction's most colorful characters.

# FIFTH VOYAGE

by WC Roberts

I drained the bottle and christened his skull
with a caravel of skin and bone
launched on Cherkee Lake, near Morristown,
where the floodwaters crested.

*7 July 1948*

The Post unrolled out of Memphis,
held with arms outstretched, become my sail
with eyes cut out or torn from the text
to serve as knotholes for voyeurs
pining for worlds to come.

I straddled his back and he carried me
spewing curses and a mouthful of red clay
across the still, green waters of youth
eyes in the sky brought down to earth
by cowbirds and swarms of black flies
along the banks of Panther Creek.

They make their deposit in bone meal and Gore
my dreams of reaching the other side
etched in stained glass by Truman
and panhellenic feats of stillborn congeniality.

After traveling the byways of East Tennessee, **WC Roberts** settled down in a mobile home up on Bixby Hill, on land that was once the county dump. The only window looks out on a ragged scarecrow standing in a field of straw and dressed in WC's own discarded clothes. WC dreams of the desert, of finally getting his first television set, and of ravens. Above all, he writes. His poetry has been published in *Illumen, Mindflights, Aoife's Kiss, Basement Stories, Labyrinth Inhabitant Magazine, Scifaikuest* and *Star\*Line,* and is forthcoming in *Space and Time Magazine* and *The Martian Wave.*

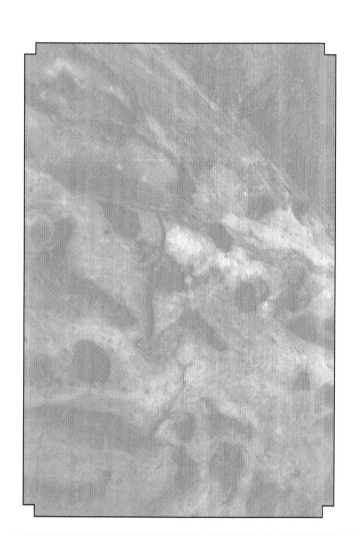

# STRANGE GOODS AND OTHER ODDITIES

## Books, Movies, Music and More

***Dismember,* by Daniel Pyle; Blood Brothers Publishing, 2009; 306 pgs.**

 Horror isn't always about monsters jumping out of the darkness or maniacs torturing innocent souls. Sometimes, when done well, horror can be about the larger issues in life that keep us grounded in everyday existence; issues of family, bereavement, and a loss of freedom. In these instances, the terror depicted on the page pulls you in and makes you shudder—not because something might leap out and grab you, but because you can see, through the written word, how fragile life can be.

*Dismember,* a fast-paced yet introspective tale of innocence lost, is one of those works. The story spans twenty-three years, from an unfortunate car accident in the mountains around Denver to the exploits of the lone survivor of said accident, one Dave Abbott, on his thirtieth birthday some years later.

Davy has grown up isolated and afraid, held captive by a sadistic and introverted mountain man named simply Mr. Boots. Not a lot of his time in seclusion is explained in the text, but you still get the feeling that Mr. Boots did certain things to little Davy that folks in civilized society would cower in the corner, cover their eyes, and shudder when presented with. I, for one, was happy with the lack of explanation. I have no need to read about a child being abused, sexually or otherwise, which the text suggests but never goes into detail about. These ugly situations are handled beautifully, with passing allusions that stick with the reader, because in many ways what we imagine in our own minds is much worse than the writer could possibly describe.

On his thirtieth birthday, Davy—now Dave—goes ahead with his plan; he will reassemble his dead family, through kidnapping and force if need be. From then on, the book follows five separate points of view: Dave; an eleven-year-old boy named Zach; and the Pullmans—Libby, Mike, and their son Trevor, a divorced family trying to find a shred of normalcy after the end of their marriage has forced each parent to cope with the emptiness of a life with no partner.

This particular aspect of the plot I found most intriguing. I loved the interplay between the two separate halves of this family unit. For once, there is a divorced couple who aren't constantly at each other's throats. They have a mutual respect for each other, though the reasons for their separation are readily apparent. They work together to raise Trevor, and neither would think about using him or their love of him as a weapon against the other. As I said, refreshing.

The corruption of purity is the overriding theme of the novel. Author Pyle brilliantly juxtaposes the horrors Dave experiences in his childhood with those of Zach and Trevor, the two boys he abducts. And Dave, himself, is a more than worthy villain. I found myself rooting for him to come to his senses, for someone to save him from himself, during different sections of the book, because I felt for him and his situation. This is a man who's still in many ways just a boy; he grew up alone, with a strange, cruel caretaker, and he only longs for the peace and comfort he'd experienced as a child. Sure, the guy is in need of years and perhaps decades of therapy, but the amount of love and caring he displays cannot be denied. This makes the violence he enacts all the more vicious. He is an emotionally stunted sociopath, and it's not his fault in the slightest.

I especially appreciated the different viewpoints within the book. The transitions from the thoughts of the children to those of the adults were well-done and believable. The kids acted and spoke like kids, and the grown-ups were satisfactorily flawed yet likeable. And the end...I won't tell you about it, because it will ruin the surprise, but let's just say it was completely unexpected, shocking, and brilliant.

*Dismember* is a fantastic read, folks. Fast-paced and at times brutal, it carries the emotional weight that makes you want to turn just one more page. It focuses on the little things and lets it sink in how much we take something as simple as taking a bath for granted. Congratulations to Daniel Pyle. He's

written something special here. It gets one heartfelt recommendation from me.

*–Robert J. Duperre*

### "Scorch Atlas" by Blake Butler; Featherproof Books, 2009; 158 pgs.

This book is a nightmare, a dark and haunting nightmare. It is a novel made up of small apocalypses, the world ending again and again, figuratively and literally. It is a shadowy view through a kaleidoscope held under water in a stagnant pond, written in thirteen or so chapters, with short stories and vignettes tied together yet totally independent of each other. The world is dead or dying. The skies are raining mud or glass, or both. People are sick, molding and swelling, dying. Their stories told in a fractured prose that blends black poeticism with a surrealist tone. It is an example of Bizarro done right.

"Smoke House" seemingly addresses the mourning process of a family who has lost a child. Several half-page pieces named for elements like "Water" and "Dust" are disturbing portraits of a world gone mad and its inhabitants trapped in the maelstrom. Hopelessness has never been painted as beautifully as in some of the pieces contained here.

The book itself is a thing to behold: gorgeous, made to look like an aged library tome complete with catalog tag on the spine. Scorch Atlas is written in a clear and artful manner. The attention to descriptive detail is flawless. It is brutal in its violence and bleak snapshot of the world as her spin begins to slow, her skin begins to sag and gray—a prophetic literary flipbook of the End Times. If you like your fiction daring and left of center, and you like to be haunted by the visuals of what you have read...*Scorch Atlas!*

*–John Boden*

### *The Scream Queen's Survival Guide,* by Meredith O'Hayre; Adams Media; 2010; 211 pgs.

 A year or so ago I reviewed a little book by Seth Grahame-Smith titled *How to Survive a Horror Movie*. This new book by Meredith O'Hayre reminds me a lot of that earlier book, and that's a very good thing. *Scream Queen* is pretty much the same idea: A humorous what-to-do, look-out-for, and how-to list for you to follow if you should ever find yourself stuck in a real-life horror movie and want to make it out alive. This time around there is a slight feminine point of view, as befitting the *Queen* in the title. But for the most part this is a good guide for both sexes when facing drooling zombies, chainsaw-wielding psychos, creepy little kids, and even the Devil himself.

In addition to the expected funny survival tips to all the old tropes used in horror flicks, the book offers a few unique tidbits along the way. Scattered throughout are sections like "My Bad: Fuck-ups on Film," where the author gives examples of gaffs and boo-boos from famous fright flicks. One of my favorites was one that I missed in the 2005 remake of *The Amityville Horror* where the stars drive over to Starbucks for a nice latte...despite the movie being set in 1975. And yet the book does make some boo-boos of its own, like when it lists *Duel* as Stephen King's first movie—it was actually Steven Spielberg's first. But hey, turnabout is fair play and all that.

There are fun and informative bits about Japanese remakes, slashers, vampires, and all sorts of bump-in-the-night boogiemen, each accompanied by survival tips and a quote from the Scream Queen herself. Furthermore, the sources are wide and deep for this book, from the creepiest of classics to the most current fright flicks, like *Daybreakers* and HBO's *True Blood* series. There's even a nice appendix of "Must-see Scary Flicks," but with such films as *Turistas* and *Urban Legends: Final Cut* on the list I've really got to question the author's horror street-cred.

If you are a horror-movie junkie like me you'll love *The Scream Queen's Survival Guide*. It's a quick, fun—and funny—read that manages to impart a fair bit of horror info and trivia along the way. If you are not a horror fan... then I don't think you're reading this anyway, but who knows, this book just might make you a fan. Weirder things have happened after all.

*–Brian M. Sammons*

**Alice (Neco z Alenky), by Jan Svankmajer (director, writer); starring Kristýna Kohoutová; 1988; Unrated; 86 min.**

Jan Svankmajer, a Czech filmmaker who has generated comparisons with David Lynch, made the leap from shorts to feature films with this surreal adaptation of Lewis Carroll's classic children's book. Kristýna Kohoutová is the only live actor in the film; the rest of the characters are animated by means of stop motion animation. Even Alice herself is an animated doll when she shrinks—a neat innovation. Svankmajer uses very little dialogue in the film, most of it being voiced by Alice as narrator, preferring to let his bizarre assembly of animated dolls, animal skeletons and stuffed animals convey the story through action. This is a major plus, since the dialogue is overdubbed from the original Czech.

Svankmajer mostly sticks to Carroll's framework, although he gives everything a darker feel. This is no Disneyfied adaptation for children. The White Rabbit is a complex character, snapping his teeth ominously while alternately running away from and chasing Alice and eating the sawdust that leaks out of him when he is injured. The caterpillar is more subtle, consisting of a stocking with false teeth and eyes. Nothing in Svankmajer's world is wholly inanimate, as scissors and even Alice's own stockings are imbued with life to suit whatever effect he has in mind.

One particularly jarring impression is created when Alice voices speech connectives such as "said the White Rabbit" and there is a close up of her mouth. The effect is enhanced by the disconnect between the overdubbed English being out of sync with the filmed Czech dialogue. It wears a bit thin by the end of the movie, but it's a fine, creepy effect all the same.

I've showed this film to several people since "discovering" it on Netflix and no one can tear their eyes away from it, even while being profoundly disturbed by the visuals. This is one film that no review can quite do justice to. I suggest you track it down and see it for yourself. You'll be glad you did.

*–Nick Contor*

*The Taint,* **by Drew Bolduc and Dan G. Nelson (directors); starring Drew Bolduc, Colleen Walsh, Kenneth Hall; 2010; Unrated; 70 min.**

I normally don't dig low-budget independent flicks. While you get the occasional pleasant surprise, far more often than not there's a reason those bargain-basement films stay underground and unknown. Quite simply, most of them aren't very good. That's why when I get a request to watch and review one of those films, I usually pass. But I do try to keep an open mind, so if a movie has a trailer I'll usually give it a look to see if I want to invest 90 minutes or so in it. That is why I watched the trailer to *The Taint*. Two minutes later I knew I had to see this movie. Why? Because it looked completely, totally, absolutely crazy. Now, I didn't know if it would be any good, but it sure looked like something I had to experience for myself. But I thought the same thing about *A Siberian Film* and *August Underground*.

That is not to say that this movie is like those others in tackling unpleasant subjects in a serious light. No. *The Taint* firmly has its tongue stapled to its cheek. All the gross, disgusting, vile things this movie does are done with a smile on its dimwitted, gapped-toothed, vacant-eyed face. It revels in its repulsiveness and thoroughly enjoys its exploitation of all things crass and icky. It is offensive, rude and crude, and it's completely fine with that.

So, have I enticed you into watching this film yet? If not, then good for you. Feel free to stop reading now and never think of this movie gain. If this does sound like a film you want to see, then God help you…but then, I felt the same way so I can't condemn you. So if you're still reading this, let's get too it.

The story, such as it is, of *The Taint* is about some scientist making a drug to give guys bigger johnsons. Something goes wrong with the drug, it gets into the water supply, and soon all the men, save our hero Phil, are killing women. And that's it for the story. But that does nothing to prepare you for what this little gem has to offer.

Things begin with our stoner hero getting chased by a bucked-toothed psycho with a scythe who craps himself in the middle of the chase—and yes, we get to see him do it. A few minutes later, Phil finds a bloody, mangled corpse and promptly vomits…a lot. Yes, we get to see that, too, and it looks like the actor—and producer, writer, director, and just about everything else—Drew Bolduc went the extra mile and puked for real. Thanks for that, Drew.

A few moments later, while Phil is taking a wicked wiz, another psycho comes out of the woods, holding a rock over his head, and with his penis sticking out of his pants, spraying semen all over the place like a sputtering garden hose. So at the five-minute mark in this film we have covered all of the bodily fluids and excretions and this flick is just getting started. What, you want more highlights? Ok, there are lots of women getting their heads caved in by rocks, a coat-hanger abortion, gallons of fake blood and semen, way too many gay jokes, vaginas vomiting out blood, sex as seen from the inside of a vagina, gratuitous nudie shots, Nazis sizing up men's schlongs and executing those who don't measure up, two different faces getting peeled off, penises getting shot and hacked off, and a cartoon about cute bunnies getting tortured in a test lab.

Sounds like a good time, right?

If you are into the mondo gory, offensive, silly, and disturbing flicks then you might dig this. If not, then you should stay the hell away from this movie. As for me, I ping-ponged back and forth. Sometimes I laughed out loud, other times I cringed, and at other times I just rolled my eyes. *The Taint* is uneven and could use some polish, to be sure, but I did admire the "Screw it, we're gonna go for it" attitude. Love it or hate it, they really don't make movies like this anymore, at least not in America.

*–Brian Sammons*

**Mistress of the Dark, by Ghoultown; Angry Planet Records, 2009; CD: 6 tracks, 24 min; DVD: 97 min.**

 On the rusty-spurred boot heels of *Life After Sundown*, **Ghoultown** returns with *Mistress of the Dark,* a hellbilly horror-fried ode to the true Mistress of the Dark, Cassandra Peterson, better known to generations of horror—and boob—fans as Elvira. The limited edition release (only 2,000 copies were pressed) includes a six-track EP and a DVD, all housed in a digipack that was brilliantly designed by artist/writer/director Gris Grimly. He also directed the DVD portion of *Mistress of the Dark.*

Conceived after Cassandra's manager heard **Ghoultown** playing a special acoustic set, and upon her personal request for an official—not to mention long overdue—theme song, bandleader Count Lyle wrote "Mistress of the Dark," a darkly swingin' and surf-rock groovin' punk tune with a killer hook. The song's tongue-in-cheek lyrics—*"What I wouldn't give, for one night, to climb those haunted hills"*—fit perfectly with Elvira's quirky persona, and it's done in such a sincere manner

that it avoids coming off as cheesy. This one is an instant classic.

(On behalf of the universe, and with no disrespect to **The Oak Ridge Boys,** thank you, Lyle!)

The EP is backed by a newly recorded version of the fan-favorite "Return of the Living Dead," from *Give 'Em More Rope.* This new version has a fuller, more in-your-face sound, with horns replacing the female harmonies that were on the original. There's also a new, very **Misfits**-like track called "My Halloween," plus the epic "Drink with the Living Dead" from *Life After Sundown.* Closing the EP are two title-track remixes, which strike me as more novelty/filler than anything. I dig bands like **KMFDM** and **Front Line Assembly,** so I like the songs, but they're not essential tracks.

The EP is worth the money alone, but there's also the DVD, the main focus of which is the video for the title track, starring none other than the Hostess with the Mostess, Elvira, and filmed in the legendary Magic Castle in Los Angeles. In addition to the video, there's a 25-minute documentary with footage of Count Lyle, Cassandra, and Gris Grimly discussing how the project came to be. There's also a video-to-storyboard comparison—which syncs up the storyboard concepts with the actual video—and a campy spoof of *Hee Haw,* the late-60s/early-70s variety show, called *Har Har.* Bad jokes, Buck Horn, the hilarious host, and **Ghoultown** performances (to studio tracks) of "Mistress of the Dark," "Find a Good Horse," and "The Ballad of Clarence Heckles," a wicked song currently only found on the companion CD to Grimly's *Cannibal Flesh Riot!* Rounding things out are four easily-found Easter eggs.

Little more need be said, really. *Mistress of the Dark* is fantastic. Sadly, despite its limited nature, there are still copies available. Please do yourself—and the band—a favor and buy a copy.

**Ghoultown,** Gris Grimly, and Elvira. Seems like a no-brainer to me.

*–K. Allen Wood*

### *Toplin,* by Michael McDowell; Abyss/Dell, 1985; 277 pgs.

When I was a teenager, I would frequent the book stores and local department stores and scour the racks for anything that may curb my hunger for horror. I bought countless pulp novels with cheesetastical covers of demons and skeletons. Some were not so good, but others stuck with me forever. This is one of those classics that I credit with helping me fall in love with horror... again. I bought this paperback when it was originally published, and read it in an evening. I loved that it was so different.

Devoid of a linear plot or traditional narrative, *Toplin* tells, in first-person, the story of an unnamed hero. The tale begins with him going to the corner market to buy an essential spice needed for a recipe—"Recipes must be followed exactly," he later explains—and follows him on a long and winding adventure that encompasses all manner of urban paranoia and serious OCD issues.

The "main character" decides it is his duty to help an unspeakably ugly waitress die. This quest then becomes more intriguing as his path crosses with a cast of strange characters. He runs into a strange street gang, comprised of two sets of identical twins, dressed to mirror one another. He meets an unusual pharmaceutical deliveryman and his elderly grandfather. Drunken truck drivers and a homeless sculptor all make appearances in this story. But the most interesting person is the teller of the tale himself. Never actually named, I always assumed him to be the Toplin of the title. He can't see colors and locks his apartment with a combination lock. He has twelve shelves of cookbooks and a closet full of identical suits numbered S-1 through S-6. He cleans in a fashion so detailed and compulsory it was OCD when OCD wasn't cool. He schedules his masturbatory practice... and his walls bleed.

If this piques your interest, then track this one down, as well as all of McDowell's other books. A gifted writer who passed away too soon, he was more widely known for his screenplay work with the *Tales from the Darkside* series and a little movie called *Beetlejuice,* but it's all about *Toplin* for me.

*–John Boden*

**The Occult Files of Albert Taylor,** by Derek Muk; Impact Books, 2009; 204 pgs.

 The great thing about short stories is that, if written well, you can't stop reading until they're done. Every word means something, and every section is important to the overall arc of the story. They can strike you in the gut, force you to think, or simply leave you speechless.

Then again, if they're not written well, you can throw out what is written above.

*The Occult Files of Albert Taylor,* a collection of eleven short stories by Derek Muk, is a perfect example of this.

This book maddened me. I kept going from story to story, thinking that the one I'd just read was simply a dud and the next would be better. With a couple exceptions, they weren't.

The only two stories that leapt out at me were *"Dear Boss,"* a tale that combines the Freemasons and the reincarnation of Jack the Ripper into a tidy little snippet of adventure, and *"The Boogeyman,"* a story in which a dimension-hopping baddie who might be some sort of demon kills kids in an abandoned tunnel.

Yet even with these two stories, the only thing that pulled me in was the subject matter, not the writing. That aspect, just as with all the other stories inside, is stiff and robotic. In fact, it reads like a poorly-constructed collection of young adult stories that R.L. Stine might have thought of and then discarded. I found myself skipping

ahead, especially with the longer tales (such as *"Footprints,"* a story about Bigfoot), which is a death knell for short fiction.

In all the stories, Albert Taylor is the main character. The problem with this, however, is that he isn't interesting. He seems to know a great deal about strange occurrences, but a chipmunk is more emotionally relevant than he is. In fact, I found his cohorts much more interesting, though even they weren't very fleshed out...or believable.

Perhaps the most painful part of this anthology, however, is the dialogue. It is so poorly constructed and stiff that it might seem as if the author has never held a conversation in his life. For example, at the beginning of one story, a young man meets up with a young lady at a local eatery. The young woman's reaction to his greeting goes as follows:

"Sorry for pigging out," she giggled. "I was starving. I eat a lot but none of it shows on my skinny frame."

Huh? Seriously? Who talks like this?

I was so bored with this book that I struggled to reach the end...but reach the end I did, and that, in itself, is an accomplishment. At first I couldn't decide if I didn't like the book because of a clash of tastes, seeing as most of these stories were previously published in magazines such as *Sinister Tales* and *Switchblade,* but after mulling it over a bit, I decided this is just a perfect example of poor writing. In other words, it's really not worth your time if you're older than twelve, and even then it's an iffy proposition.

*–Robert J. Duperre*

### *They Had Goat Heads,* by D. Harlan Wilson; Atlatl Press, 2010; 135 pgs.

The deliriously bizarre writings of D. Harlan Wilson have become a personal favorite of mine within the last year, beginning when I purchased the two-volume *Bizarro Start Kit.* In *They Had Goat Heads* Wilson continues to do what he does best, which is paint sometimes abrupt and always bizarre pictures of everyday situations gone down the rabbit hole...most never going beyond a page or two in length, some just a sentence long.

I think my favorite of the bunch is the dire tale *"The Sister."* It has the honor of being the only illustrated piece in the book, and that eerie narrative and unique art style meld to create an unforgettable thing.

If you don't appreciate the Bizarro movement, or the less than linear subject matter of some of the fringe authors out there, then *They Had Goat Heads* will not appeal to you. However, if you like things that are off-kilter and unusual, vicious wordplay and high octane assault with a deadly vocabulary...D. Harlan may just be your poster boy.

*–John Boden*

### *Pieces,* by Juan Piquer Simón (director), Dick Randall and John Shadow (screenplay); starring Christopher George, Lynda Day George, Frank Braña; 1982; Unrated; 87 min.

This weird, weird, freakin' WEIRD movie is one of my all-time favorite slasher flicks, and not because it's a great film. No. It is far from that, and yet it is not laughably bad either, like so many other "crazy killer" flicks that I can't stand to watch. For me, *Pieces* exists in a world of its own. It's got lots of blood and naked woman (the staples of all good slashers), but it takes so many trips into far leftfield that it leaves you scratching your head or laughing out loud. This Spanish film, with many English-speaking actors, is one import not to be missed by fans of off-the-wall splatter flicks. And at long last the mad geniuses over at Grindhouse Releasing have given it the two-disc special-edition DVD treatment it deserves. So let's dive into the pure insanity of *Pieces.*

The story begins with a little boy putting together a jigsaw puzzle with a nude girl on it. Mom catches him and freaks out. The boy tops his mother's freak-out with one of his own, except his involves an axe—and her face. Many years later, the story picks up at a college where the same boy, now all grown up, wants to make his own naked woman jigsaw puzzle. So naturally he breaks out a chainsaw and starts collecting limbs from all of the lovely coeds. Oh, and then a girl on a skateboard crashes to her death through a mirror two moving men were holding up across a sidewalk. What, you didn't expect that? Well that's what makes this movie great; you never see what's coming: a woman walking alone on the campus at night suddenly getting attack by a Bruce Lee impersonator who, after three minutes of punching and kicking at the air, says sorry and goes on his merry way; or the killer sneaking into a tiny elevator with a potential victim, his chainsaw hidden from her by holding it in one hand behind his back; or the amazing way actress Linda Day George delivers the line, "That bastard! Bastard! BASTARD!" Honestly, this is one of those rare movies that descriptions really can't do it justice; it must be experienced firsthand to be properly appreciated.

A different version of *Pieces* came out on DVD a few years back, but that edition was pretty horrible. The picture and sound was bad and it had no special features whatsoever. Thankfully, Grindhouse Releasing swooped in to save the day. This reviewed edition gives us the movie uncut, so it's packed with gallons of blood and gore. And what good are buckets of blood if it doesn't look good? The picture and sound have both been beautifully restored, and there are some new and very cool special features on the discs: There's an audio track recorded during a live screening of the movie at the Vine Theater in Hollywood, so you can get the full theater-going experience. Also, a Spanish soundtrack, if you want to hear the film as it first came out. Interviews with the director and genre

star Paul L. Smith, who plays the crazy campus caretaker. A few hidden Easter eggs—there's a great one with noted horror director Eli Roth—and in this day of opening up a DVD case to find only a disc inside and nothing more, Grindhouse has included a mini poster and liner notes by horror historian and author Chas Balun. With all this love shown to it, Grindhouse Releasing has set the bar pretty damn high on how a little DVD releasing company can take a cult classic and do it like it was a multi-million-dollar-making movie.

As I said at the start, I love this major-league weird movie. If you're a slasher fan with tastes as warped as mine then I know you will, too. Do yourself a favor and pick up a copy.

*–Brian Sammons*

*Jacob's Ladder,* **by Adrian Lyne (director) and Bruce Joel Rubin (writer); starring Tim Robbins, Elizabeth Peña, Danny Aiello; 1990; R; 113 min.**

It's been twenty years since this classic film of psychological horror was released, but it was a movie that had a history going back more than thirty years. Bruce Joel Rubin wrote the original screenplay in 1980, but resisted interest from traditional horror directors and overcame objections from mainstream Hollywood. The script gained a reputation as one of the best unproduced scripts in Hollywood while Rubin held on to it until he was confident it would receive the treatment he wanted for it.

Eventually, Adrian Lyne signed on to direct and gave *Jacob's Ladder* a nightmarish feel that few horror films ever attain, blending what appears to be dream and reality so successfully that it is often difficult to tell them apart. He pioneered the shaking-head effect later used in films like *The Ring* and *Silent Hill,* and still did it best, in my opinion. The demonlike creatures that plague Jacob Singer are among the most effective and creepy images ever filmed, and Tim Robbin's vulnerable portrayal draws the audience into his visions, and whether real or imagined makes little difference. The film's final twist, while not totally original, is deftly done and anyone with a suspension of disbelief will be fooled on first viewing. I was.

It's likely that most if not all *Shock Totem* readers will already be familiar with this classic. It is a prime example of Hollywood's failure to recognize good original writing, and illustrative of how those limitations are worsening with time. For a few years now, there have been discussions aimed at remaking this film, but to what end? Will they improve on the original film? It seems unlikely to me.

What is sought is a quick payoff, a cheap and easy remake that will net a profit while ultimately degrading the legacy of a truly great film. It is a theme that we see played out more and more each day, and one reason why the film industries in other countries are gaining the respect that Hollywood once had—but is selling off a piece at a time like an aging hooker.

I have to believe that there are other original scripts like *Jacob's Ladder* out there that filmmakers are ignoring; preferring to make an easy buck rather than taking a risk on an unknown product. It's a shame.

*—Nick Contor*

### The Butcher Bride, by Vince Churchill; Black Bed Sheet Books, 2009; 275 pgs.

There is a delicate balance you need to obtain when violence against women is the driving aspect of a novel. I have read and seen many examples of this over the years. The hideousness becomes the focal point of the tale and it is disgusting. There is something inherently vile about sexual abuse, especially of women and children, and the use of rape as a major plot device can register anywhere from irresponsible to downright evil.

Needless to say, when I started reading *The Butcher Bride,* by Vince Churchill, and discovered that a gang rape at a Halloween party in the beginning of the book is the impetus for everything that comes later, I was more than a little wary.

Luckily, author Churchill handles these events with uncommon sensitivity. He gives us just enough description to get the point across, and allows the reactions of the victims to guide the tale. Yes, there is revenge here—the tortured woman, Marlie Downing, a girl who's grown up as a servant in the mansion of a rich family in Indiana, ends up slicing and dicing multiple partygoers, and is then dispatched by the man of her dreams, who is also the cause of her brutal and perverse attack—but this is only part of the story.

After these horrible events, the story jumps thirty years. It is Halloween again, the anniversary of the killings at the Silas estate. The mansion, which has been vacant since the day of the slaughter, is turned into a famous murder house, and the Butcher Bride, as the deceased Marlie is dubbed, becomes a local celebrity. Numerous researchers and other intrigued parties have been killed in freak accidents in the mansion over the last thirty years, helping to grow the house's—and therefore the town's—legend.

Enter Stuart and Evie, a young and adventurous couple who rent out the mansion for the weekend. Evie is the daughter of a famous Hollywood producer with a serious hard-on for serial killers, especially our poor, insane Marlie Downing. Is it a smart move? Not really, considering the mansion's reputation. But history is overflowing with tales of smart people shirking advice and doing stupid things. Stuart and Evie definitely fall into this category.

This is where the story takes a turn. It becomes a combination haunted house/'80s slasher flick. There are numerous deaths, all thanks to the ghosts of Marlie and her depraved victims. The action is fast-paced, gruesome, and charged with disturbing sexual energy, but just as with everything else in the book, Churchill is delicate when handling these situations. Never is violence celebrated, and not once is

an individual's death presented in an off-handed manner.

Despite being a story that revolves around a mass murderer, the victims aren't forgotten. As a matter of fact, that point is made abundantly clear in the middle of the novel. It's an interesting study of how we as a society look at death, how we celebrate the disquieting events in life as long as they don't "affect us." I appreciated it wholeheartedly, and wish more horror writers would be as astute.

I cannot go any further without discussing the relationship that begins the whole mess between Marlie and Michael Silus, heir to the family fortune and object of Marlie's desire. Michael's father is dominating and vindictive, traits he passes down to his son. The elder Silas, though married, held Marlie's mother, the head of the mansion staff, as a mistress for many years. And Marlie carries on with her matriarch's habits, forming an addicting sexual bond with the son that she thinks will lead to a future as Mrs. Michael Silas. Given the history of the family and the debauchery that occurs within the mansion walls, is at any wonder she would? It isn't until Michael's doomed fiancée orders him to cut things off that the plan for the brutal sexual attack—formulated by a most unexpected party—comes to pass.

I found it interesting that Michael is tainted and commanding sexually, just like his father. Sex, when looked at from a certain point of view, is all about power. It's about seeing something you want and taking it. It makes sense that the Silas's, with their life of prosperity, would want to snatch up as much influence as possible. Marlie also falls into line with this thinking. She grew up in the house and wanted nothing more than to have Michael for her own. Yes, she is a victim, but in a way she is a *willing* victim, just as twisted and damaged as the people she murders.

In all, I had a blast reading *The Butcher Bride.* Churchill creates a fun world that we can easily pass off as fantasy, and yet does an amiable job of interspersing an important message into his words. The climax is apropos, and everyone involved gets what's coming to them. In fact, if I had one complaint about the book, it would be that I knew how it would end in the first fifty pages. But that's okay. The journey is what matters, and in this particular novel, it's one hell of a fun ride.

*The Butcher Bride* can be obtained at vincechurchill.com.

*–Robert J. Duperre*

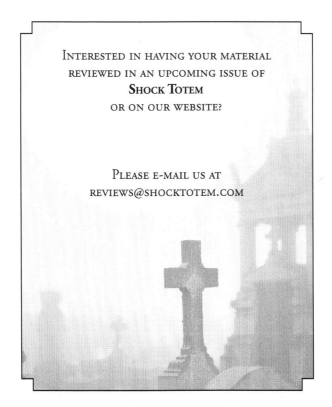

Interested in having your material
reviewed in an upcoming issue of
**Shock Totem**
or on our website?

Please e-mail us at
reviews@shocktotem.com

# ABOMINATIONS
# VORACIOUS BLACK

## by Mercedes M. Yardley

The darkness has teeth.

As children, we knew it. We were terrified of sleeping in our rooms alone. Afraid of the monsters that lived in our closets with toothy smiles that wrapped most of the way around their heads. Scared of the things that lived under our beds, knowing they would scrape their claws against our skin if our leg slipped out from under the covers. Our mothers and fathers reassured us that nothing lived in the dark that wasn't in the light, but we knew this wasn't true. As adults we park our cars under streetlights. We're attracted to brightly lit neon signs. Pictures from space show that as soon as darkness spreads across the earth, the lights flick on. We're still frightened.

When I was in college, my friend, whom I shall call Anne, and I studied mines for a geology project. Anne's father was a miner, and one day we received special permission to don mining gear and follow him into the Earth for an hour. "Darkness demands respect, girls," he said. "Don't move. Stay exactly where you are. Ready?"

We were ready. We weren't afraid. We were strong, independent girls and the darkness wasn't anything to be afraid of. I'd been telling myself this for years. After all, Anne's father was there, his teeth shining white under his dark mustache. The rest of the team was there, as well. What could a little dark do?

We nodded. Anne's father shouted something and the crew shouted something back. Then the lights went off.

The sheer power of the darkness made me suck in my breath. It was thick and heavy, weighty, like oil or mist. Every childhood fear I thought I'd outgrown came slithering back. Somebody shifted their footing and it echoed eerily throughout the unfamiliar mine. My eyes strained so hard for the tiniest source of light that they physically hurt. But there was nothing to see, just the absolute absence of light. Just the hunger and the possibilities. I reminded myself that I was an adult now, that this wasn't real terror, that I only had to hold on for another five seconds. Four...three...two...one...

The lights came back on and suddenly I could breathe again. I turned away, lifted my mask, and discretely wiped at the corners of my eyes with my sleeve.

Anne's father looked at us and laughed. He pointed and I realized that Anne and I had both grabbed each other's gloved hands in the dark. We separated, feeling a little bit silly. But later that night, back in the safety of Anne's room, she slammed down her pen.

"I was so scared," she told me.

I nodded. "I am never, never going back in another mine."

There was something I didn't tell her, though. There was a reason why I was so heavily affected, why I stood there in the cold darkness begging for the lights to go on. It's something that we don't really talk about in my hometown.

I'm from a blue-collar desert town. There aren't a lot of us, and we stick together to overcome the harsh conditions. The town is basically divided into two main occupations: coal miners and power-plant workers. My daddy is a plant worker. His daddy was a plant worker. You go where the job is, and if the job leaves you out in the middle of nowhere, so be it. There aren't many places more rural than my hometown. It still doesn't have a traffic light. It's full of charm and dust and grit.

But when I was five, tragedy struck. There was a massive fire in the Wilberg Mine, and while one miner managed to escape, twenty-seven people were killed when their escape route was cut off. They were daddies, too. Granddaddies. Brothers. One of the victims was the first woman to die in a mine since women were allowed inside.

Twenty-seven people in such a small town means that everybody was touched. We just shut down for a while after that. Friends couldn't come over and play because we were being "respectful." I couldn't go to some of their houses because their mommies were still crying and couldn't get out of bed. My mother baked cakes and loaves of fresh bread. She wrapped them up, put them in my red Radio Flyer, and we walked around town, dropping them off at certain houses. I remember thinking that homemade bread from a neighbor must be able to heal any wound. I was too young to know any better.

When I was about eight, I was walking downtown with an ice cream in my hand. I saw a friend curled up next to the mine memorial, crying. I offered her my ice cream, but I didn't know what to say.

Years later she mentioned that she had nightmares of her Old Daddy showing up, his skin charred and cracked, just when she was hugging her New Daddy. She wasn't betraying either of them, both were good, kind men who were wonderful fathers, but you can't explain these feelings to a child.

That is what I thought about when Anne and I were in the mine together. That is why I swore I'd never step foot inside one again.

But Anne did. She started working in a mining control-room. She fell in love with a man there and they were married. They worked together for several years.

"It isn't as scary as it used to be," she told me once. "Are you sure you wouldn't like to come inside some day?"

"Never," I told her. I was surprised at the venom in my voice. "Never, never, never!"

Then one August, her husband quit his job. I'm not exactly sure why, because suddenly it seemed unimportant. The very next day the mine collapsed. His team was inside. He wasn't.

"I should be in there," Anne's husband had said, sitting at home with his head in his hands. "Those are my men. Those are my friends."

Six miners were trapped. I knew every one of them or their families. My mother was the one who called with the news. I remember dropping the phone on the floor after she told me.

Even though I now live several states away, my soul is still tied to that town. The desert runs in my veins. What happens there deeply affects me. Those are my people. They're my lifeblood.

I know how dark a mine can be. The horror I had felt on that calm day in college, gripping Anne's hand in the dark of the mine, her father beside us, was almost more than I could stand. That's when we were without light for ten seconds. What would it be like to be trapped for days? To be crushed under the rubble? How did those brave men feel when they heard everything come down around them? If I'm thinking of this, and I'm only a friend, how do their families feel? What screams through their minds when they turn their thoughts to their trapped loved ones?

Signs went up immediately after the collapse. "Pray For Our Miners." "Don't Give Up Hope." "We Love You." Children tied yellow ribbons to school fences. Friends, families, and reporters gathered at the site of the mine and in living rooms to monitor the desperate rescue efforts. Every little action was reported. I was glued to the news channel, riveted to the Internet, constantly on the phone. My heart hurt. My soul was in anguish. It brought up old wounds I thought were long—I hate to say the word—buried. But these wounds were suddenly ripped open. I wished I was five years old again, when I knew that the Big Bad had happened but I wasn't fully cognitive of it. Grief is too heavy to handle as an adult.

It took three days to bore a hole into the mine. They lowered a microphone down, and everyone held their breath.

The silence was devastating.

*What does this mean?* we wondered. It means, we told each other, that the miners retreated to a different part of the mine. It means they were exhausted and conserving their energy. That's all. It couldn't possibly be anything else.

They took samples of the air and declared it livable. That's what we focused on. We ignored the implications of that chilling silence.

More samples showed that the earlier conclusion was incorrect. The air was, in fact, fatal. The spine of the entire town seemed to bend and slump.

But we are not quitters. We don't just give up. The search rescue continued, although I think we all knew that it had by then turned into a recovery mission. Still, nobody said it aloud. Not people from the town, anyway. The outsiders did that. Reporters. Family that flew in. People who didn't understand that when things are at their darkest, you have to keep going. If you stop, you fall—and if we fell at that point, I don't know if we'd have been able to get back up.

Then there was a second collapse. Three of the rescue workers were killed. I still remember hearing the words: "The rescue has been called off." I put my hands over my face and cried. *We abandoned them.* That's how I feel. Although I realize that you can't trade the lives of the living for the dead, we still left them to have their marrow sucked out by the dark.

I think Anne's husband broke a little that day. He hadn't been sleeping. He hadn't been eating, or talking to anybody. He felt that he should have been in there with his team—but he was grateful he wasn't. That, of course, made him feel worse. He didn't want to hear things like "It's all for the best" or "Trust in the Lord" or "Sometimes bad things happen to good people." He didn't want to hear that his reactions were normal and he would get through it. The term "survivor's guilt" sounded small and patronizing to him. He was racked. He was screaming inside. He shut down. Hopelessness is unbearably heavy.

The "Pray For Our Miners" sign stayed up. It was ripped and faded by the wind, but nobody had the heart to pull it down. The relentless sun blanched the yellow ribbons into the color of bone. They were slowly untied, one by one.

Eventually they sealed the entrances to that part of the mine. The bodies of my friends are entombed there. I think about it whenever I drive by. Whenever I can, I take a different route in order to avoid it. It's been three years and it's still too raw.

Anne still works for the mine. So does her father. I hope that her husband hasn't gone back to work there, but sometimes there isn't a choice in a small town. We lose and we mourn and we rail against our fate, and then all we can do is pick up our gear. Take a deep breath. Head back into the waiting darkness, and try to avoid its teeth.

**Mercedes M. Yardley** wears red stilettos and poisonous flowers in her hair. She often writes about the real and imagined terrors that she comes across. Her work has been published in such places as *The Vestal Review, Pedestal Magazine, Flash Fiction Online, Werewolves and Shape Shifters: The Beast Within* and *The Rambler*. She is currently working on a nonfiction book about her son's rare genetic condition, which is its own type of quiet horror.

# Day Job

by Merrilee Faber

### LEAVE NO TRACE

The doorknob was covered in blood, and slipped in my hand as I tried to turn it. I found a towel and wiped the doorknob clean. Now I had a bloody towel, a wrecked flat and a looming disaster on my hands.

I opened the door to the living room. There was blood on the walls. Blood on the furniture. Artistic red splatters on the cheap acrylic carpet.

"Leave no trace" was the first thing they told you, when your wings were shiny and new. Make it a clean disappearance. Anything left behind is an anchor to this world that the damned can use to return.

Well, they never said anything about skinny old paedophiles like Lester, who put up a fight that left us both bleeding. That was something you found out after you'd been on the job for a while, how strongly people cling to life.

What had he called me? One of God's whores. But I had done my job and sent him down.

I stepped back into a patch of sodden carpet that squelched under my boot and winced. There was no way I could clean up this mess. I stripped to my skin, leaving my bloody clothes in a pile with the towel. My boots I took into the kitchen and scrubbed and scrubbed.

I used matches and a candle, rather than holy fire, to set the flat alight. I placed the candle under the ragged curtains and stepped back. They blazed up, leaving a sooty patch on the wall.

The fire spread slowly across the carpet, inching forward until it reached the table. It licked at the varnish, dashing up the legs to dance across the top.

The smoke alarms went off. I walked out into the hall, slipped out of my humanity then stepped through the wall into the next flat.

An old woman in dressing gown and slippers was shoving things into a shopping bag. Pictures, knick-knacks, a collection of spoons. An old man hurried into the room, papers clutched to his chest.

"I've got the insurance, Faye, come on!"

"Wait, my mother's music box! It's in the bedroom cupboard!"

"Leave it!" He hauled her out, shedding paraphernalia and weeping. Smoke rushed into the room when they opened the front door and I could hear her wailing all the way down the steps.

I went to open the bedroom door to help the fire spread. Glass crunched beneath my boot. I'd stepped on one of the pictures the old woman had dropped; a faded, sepia-toned shot of a fat kid on a rocking horse. A son, I guessed. The walls were covered in photos of him, chronicling the minutiae of his life.

I followed the story. Baby, toddler, fat kid on a trike, skinny kid in a lifesaver's togs, pimply teenager. The largest photo hung above a shelf crowded with shells. A young man in uniform. Queensland Police Academy, Class of '84.

There were no more photos after that.

Something exploded, washing me with flames and curling the pictures in their frames. Sirens wailed in the street outside. I'd done enough.

I walked home through the suburbs, the afternoon air hot and sticky on my skin. People would brush against me, turn and look, see for a moment something that they could never understand, never comprehend: Beauty that was as far beyond them as the stars.

And then they would forget.

Back at my flat, I showered, pulled on jeans, shirt and humanity, and headed for work. The apartment owner was downstairs, rewiring the light over the door, which blew every time it rained. He looked up at me and smiled. Behind his round face, the soft dark stain of a sinner.

"Oh hey, Sandy, I didn't know you were in. Off to work?"

"Yep." I pulled the gate closed behind me.

## ANCHORED

I work night-shift at the post office, watching the big machines sort mail, catching the occasional letter that the machines can't process. Making enough money to pay the rent.

Everyone who works here is cut off from life. Living in the dark, sleeping in the light. Some of us have wings.

Liz didn't. She had two kids, a drinking problem, and a black stain on her soul. I didn't look closer.

If Liz ended up on a work order, it wouldn't be posted by me. Liz was the closest thing to a friend that I had. It's hard to make friends when all you can see is imperfection.

Liz waved at me and pulled on her hygiene cap. "Hey kid, how's the love life?"

"What love life?"

Same joke, every day. Liz thought I was twenty. I knew she was 32, single, living on the dole and lying about working at the post office.

The shift started and we settled to the routine. Liz talked nonstop, about her kids, her neighbours, her "loser ex," her manipulative mother. I let the words wash over me.

Anchored to humanity was what they called it. Working here, among humans, was supposed to remind us what humanity was. Because after a while, all you saw were the stains. You stopped seeing the faces they belonged to.

Liz paused in the middle of a rant about her social worker. "Can you smell smoke?"

I sniffed. "Yeah." I sniffed again. Surely the smell of the fire wasn't still clinging? I'd showered, I had on clean clothes. I stepped away from the machine and sniffed again. Still that faint tang.

Liz hit the emergency stop button. Fire in the sorting warehouse could very quickly turn into a big deal.

The supervisor lumbered over. "What's up?"

"I can smell smoke," said Liz. "Might be a letter caught."

"Or another dead mouse."

We circled the machine like a pack of dogs sniffing out a bitch, but couldn't pinpoint the location.

"Sandy, your shoe!" Liz pointed at my feet.

I looked down. A wisp of smoke curled up from under the sole of my right boot. My workboots. I clawed frantically at the laces.

"Look out. *Get back!*" But like a flock of sheep they just stood and stared dumbly.

I caught the after-image flash of wings as Wes, one of my brethren, charged over to us.

"Go!" He shoved his way through the human ring, pushing people away. "Sandy, get—"

A sound like rock tearing and then white hot brightness that hurt like fuck. I saw Wes flying backwards, a black figure in roiling clouds of flame. I pushed myself up. Everything was on fire, the machines, the letters, the walls, the air. A pair of disembodied legs twisted in the heat. I only knew they were Liz's because of the blue pants, charring into ash.

Then the flames were gone. In the crackling silence, a crash as Wes pushed himself out from under a twisted pile of shelving. We were the only living things in the factory. Ash fell around us like rain.

Wes shouted a warning. I felt a hand clamp around my throat from behind, fingers burning into my flesh.

I manifested, wings going from thought to reality and catapulting me into the thick air. The burning fingers dug deeper but the demon weighed nothing at all. Then Wes slammed into me and the three of us tumbled to the ground.

I pushed up and came face to face with Lester Carmichael, convicted paedophile, lately sent to hell. By me.

The skinny old bastard looked the same, sagging skin, thinning hair. But the watery blue eyes now snapped with power and the wrinkled skin looked like rhino hide.

"Hello, Sandy," he said.

I threw myself sideways and upwards, trying to get some distance, but he grabbed my ankle and slammed me back down again.

Wes dived toward him. Lester met him with a fist, sending Wes through a ruined sorting machine like it was made of paper.

"Go! Get help," I shouted.

Wes leaped into the air and dove through the shattered remains of a window.

"You botched the job, Sandy," said Lester.

I'd botched it all right. I edged around him. All my careful cleanup and, like a rookie, I'd scrubbed my boots instead of burning them. I wasn't even that fond of the boots; I just hated shopping for new ones. I could never find a comfortable pair in my size.

"You're not going to be popular with your manager."

"He's forgiving, didn't you hear?"

"Even so, this is a demotion for sure. Wouldn't you rather have a new start? Easy hours, all the perks?"

So the rumours were true. Downstairs was looking for new blood, and was poaching from our side. "Thanks, but no thanks. I'm not keen on the contract."

"But you've been noticed, Sandy. You're making trouble for the boss. We'd much rather have you on our side."

So it was *our side* now. I wondered what Lester had traded for his new position. Small-time paedophiles didn't get a contract, they just got an eternity. Lester had come back with more power than his insignificant life should have bought him.

"I told you, no deal." I heard the sound of wings from outside. "Now get back where you belong before we send you there, express."

The remaining windows imploded as Wes returned with our brethren. I tried to leap up to join them, but Lester-returned was faster. Stronger. He grabbed my ankle, I slammed into the ground, felt the pressure in my head as a gate opened. Lester's hand closed around my throat, and I smelled his burning breath as he leaned down.

"Do you know what they do to your kind in hell?"

The mortal plane dissolved like sugar crystals in water.

## CHANGE

Everything faded after a few years. The torture. The loss of my wings. I remember lying on a stone floor, and wondering how the stone could be so cold when the air was so hot. I hadn't seen anyone for a long time.

They made me walk to the meeting. I stood before him. Maybe I kneeled. I don't remember.

Then another voice, hot and triumphant, dictating the duties and responsibilities of my new position. Terms and conditions. One-hundred-year contract.

I don't remember signing my name. I do remember that my wing stubs itched like crazy.

## FIRST DAY

I took the bus to my first assignment. I don't drive, it's too hard to remember there are people on the roads. I could zone out on the bus, think about things.

On a whim I got off three blocks early and walked. I passed the place where the sorting warehouse used to be. There was a park there now, the trees still only knee high. A memorial stone in the centre reminded people that 26 postal workers had died there in a fire.

Every flat surface of the memorial was covered in graffiti.

The client's house was at the top of a hill, a flashy McMansion looking over the river toward the city. I knocked on the door. I was shown to the lounge by a lackey and told to wait.

I was looking out through the windows when a voice from behind startled me.

"You're not what I was expecting."

I turned. Pin-up body with a pretty-boy smile. Not at all like my previous assignments.

"What were you expecting?" Out of habit I looked for his soul, but I was blind now, I could only see the outside. Part of me relaxed.

"Someone stronger. Nowhere near as pretty."

"I'll surprise you."

"I'd like that. I'm David, by the way."

"I know."

"Of course. But I don't know your name."

"No, you don't." I glared at him. "Give me your hand."

He walked over to me and held out his hand, every move sensuous and inviting. I grabbed his hand, bit down, swallowed some blood. The stubs of my wings burned like ice. I didn't need to look at his face to know he was enjoying it. "Now get."

"For how long?" He cradled his hand, the blood pooling in his palm.

"A week." I doubted my job would take more than a day, but I didn't want to be here when he got back.

He left, taking his people with him. When the house was empty, I sank into the couch. I let his blood run through my veins, mingle with mine. The trap was set.

There was a stone sculpture by the window, abstract and featureless. Water ran down the sides to tinkle into a bowl below, filling the room with sound. I found the switch and turned it off.

I was tempted to shut myself off, too, let time flash by, but I didn't want to be caught unawares. So I sat in the flow of time and waited for the sound of wings.

I heard them, and knew there were two. That was different. We always used to work alone. Maybe the brethren had made some changes. Maybe I had been the cause.

The angels floated in through the wall, two young rookies sent to deal with an easy assignment. They stopped, confused, feeling David's blood close by but not seeing him.

They were dead before they even knew I was there.

I left them on the rug because it amused me. David would walk over them day after day and never see them. Maybe he would catch a glimpse of beauty, a flash of wings. Maybe he would feel a moment's grief and wonder why.

Maybe they would drive him crazy, eat at him until he took his own life to escape their presence.

I didn't care.

I sat on the veranda and watched the sun go down behind the city.

**Merrilee Faber** lives in the sand and fly-infested west of Australia. When not defending her family from Australia's deadly fauna, she tries to earn a crust by telling people what to do, with moderate success. She is a consummate liar, but gets away with it by calling it "fiction."

Merrilee blogs at **notenoughwords.wordpress.com**.

# A Birth in the Year of the Miracle Plague

by Jeremy Kelly

You've got to stop going around and taking other people's stuff," Moo-ma said, shaking her head as she snapped on a pair of surgical gloves she had scavenged from the old hospital. "It's not right and you know it."

The necklace was worth it though, even if Leper only got to hold it for a while. It was a pretty necklace. Well, the chain was rusted out like everything else in the world, but the jewel at the end of it was green. Like blades of grass after some rain.

Back when there used to be grass and rain.

They stayed in some rooms on the fifth floor of a building that used to be across the street from a park. It was one of those parks in a neighborhood you know your momma and daddy could never afford but they took you there sometimes so you could go somewhere nice every once in a while. That was before the war turned the world into newspaper and ash.

Leper and Moo-ma lived in two adjoining rooms. She slept in one with the strangers that came to spend the night sometimes. Leper stayed in the other, which had a section of wall blown out from the war. When he got up in the morning and there wasn't a whole lot of chemical fog, he could see a pretty good view of the city sprawling out beneath him and the twirling smoke from everybody's camp fires.

Leper sat in an old grey stool in his room and looked out at the night city while Moo-ma stood over him with a paper mask on her face and a big fresh roll of bandages in her hand. "Well you're a sight," she said and looked down at him with those momma eyes. "We're going to have to clean you up and change your bandages again. Looks like they drug you through the dirt for miles this time."

He looked down at himself. She was right. Rosa Lee had beaten him good. His t-shirt was smeared with ash and dirt and his cut-off blue jeans were worse. All of his bandages were torn or unraveled from his head to his sleeves down to his knees. He got a few good looks at the skin underneath, which he never liked to see. He had worn the bandages ever since he was born in the year of the Miracle Plague—they covered every inch of his body except for his one good eye.

Moo-ma pulled the shirt over his head and unbuttoned his pants and pulled them to the floor. She started at the top with the old bandages and unwound them down to his ankles. Leper thought that Rosa had done a pretty number on his nose. He looked at Moo-ma's eyes as she took away the bloody bandage, but she just smiled and wasn't shocked or anything. That meant nothing, he knew, because Moo-ma was sweeter to him than anyone else in the world, and if his nose was a sight she wouldn't let on.

"Those stitches on your lips holding up good?" Moo-ma asked.

He nodded.

"Good. You can breathe comfortable?"

He shrugged, and whistled through the hole in his mouth.

"Good."

When Leper was stripped down, she took the dirty bandages into the other room and came back with a pail of hot water that she had boiled on the wood stove. It had cooled down just enough now. Leper made a low sound in the back of his throat and shook his head. Moo-ma said, "Now Joshua, you know we have to get you cleaned up good, or you're going to itch." She was the only one that ever called him by his real name. She set the pail down beside him and picked out a sponge dripping with cloudy water. "I'll be gentle, baby. Promise."

When it was over, Moo-ma bandaged him back up with the fresh roll and she held him for a while until there was a knock on the door in the other room. "Love you, baby," she said. "Don't come into my room for a while. I'll come get you. And remember—if anything happens, run away from any strangers." And she left him there on the dirty pile of blankets in the corner that made up his bed.

~

Leper lay for a long while. He didn't know what sleep was because it had never happened to him before. So he thought about Daddy.

He had never met him. Moo-ma said that Daddy came along after the war. He'd been in the fighting. Toward the end of it all, he came down with the Miracle Plague like so many others.

Lots of people got it. Lots of people died. Then they came back. At first it was a miracle. Then it wasn't.

Leper listened to the muffled sounds of Moo-ma and the stranger on the other side of the apartment wall. She sounded like he was working her pretty hard, but she didn't sound like she was hurting. She was a big woman, and she was good at making them think that she enjoyed it.

That's how Daddy had come along. By the time he had his way with her, the Miracle Plague had already taken him and brought him back. Leper had seen corpses of folks who had gone and come back. He couldn't see why Moo-ma would let something like that work on her. Then again, she loved Leper for what he was, and he was half his Daddy.

After a long time Leper heard the apartment door swing open and shut. Moo-ma shuffled into his room and lay next to him smiling and smelling like somebody else's sweat. She held out a closed fist in front of Leper's fresh-bandaged face. "I've got something for you."

Leper peered up at her with his one good eye before pushing himself up on his elbows. She opened her hand and he let out a long whistle from the hole in his mouth. It was a blue marble, blue as an ocean in the picture books. He held out his hand and she dropped it in his palm. He held it up between thumb and forefinger and marveled at it with his wide lidless eye.

"Do you love it, Joshua?"

He nodded and whistled again. Yes.

"Now there's no need to go taking things that belong to others when Moo-ma can bring home some colors of the world every once in a while."

Leper carefully flipped the corner of his blanket aside and pulled a faded grey cigar box from beneath it. He sat the box on his lap and opened the lid carefully, placing the marble inside. He smiled at all of the rest of his things that had captured some of the colors of the old world, and he held each one up for her to see. Like she had never seen them before.

A bent postcard of a red strawberry. A green piece of glass. An ebony comb. A silver harmonica. A yellow pencil. Moo-ma smiled and looked at each and every one as if it were her first time ever seeing it. Like it was someone else who had given Leper these little mysteries.

They stayed awake and talked late into the night.

~

During the day the children of the city ran its streets while everyone else slept in safety with the daylight. The threw rocks through windows and they picked through the piles of garbage and rubble in the streets. They shit on the sidewalks and they pissed in the gutters. They ran with each other, they ran after each other. They beat each other bloody, and they fucked each other numb, and they did that very badly because they were too young and no one had taught them about proper lovemaking because it had left the world along with all its colors years ago.

Leper ran because it made him feel alive. Because he was always one foot in the grave. Because there was nothing else.

He left Moo-ma at the apartment at dawn. A group of strangers had shown up with a couple of gallons of fresh water. He kept to his particular borough, as did most of the kids in the city, so he knew most of them by name. He ran around a corner and found Pinky and Ira throwing rocks through a large square department-store window cut into the face of a skyscraper.

"Hey, Leper," Pinky said. "You got creamed yesterday. You got to keep your hands to yourself. Especially you."

Unlike everybody else in the world, Pinky still had a little color in her cheeks. She wasn't a big girl like Rosa Lee, but she was fat and she looked like she was blushing all of the time. She was a nice girl, all things considered.

Ira was very thin and said nothing in the way of salutations. He pulled his old brown ball-cap down over his eyes and turned his back to Leper to throw a rock.

"What are you thinking, anyhow? Going after Rosa Lee's shit," Pinky said. "You're lucky she didn't kill you."

Leper shrugged his shoulders and, with his bandaged finger, cut a mock swath across his throat from ear to ear. He hung his head to one side and slumped his shoulders, and if he could he would have stuck his tongue out, too.

Pinky laughed. "That's right," she said. "You're pretty much halfway there already."

Leper liked Pinky because she at least talked to him sometimes. He wasn't sore that she didn't step in to help when he was getting creamed by Rosa Lee. She was a big girl, but Rosa was big-boned and mad as a dog. No, he wasn't sore at all.

Ira picked up a big rock from a large pile of rubble and heaved it through the department-store window. It fell in daggered shards to the pavement. The kids stood there and watched for a moment. Leper walked toward the opening.

"Careful with all the glass," Pinky said.

Leper whistled over his shoulder in reply.

"Why we got to hang out with that kid?" Ira said.

"Shut up," Pinky replied. "You don't like it, go run around with some other kids and get your ass beat to hell."

Ira shoved his hands in the pockets of his corduroy trousers and shut up. He was just a little guy.

Leper climbed into the window and walked around inside. The department store had been sacked. Rusted racks for clothing lay overturned on the floor. Old jewelry cases lay smashed and empty. Faded dollar bills lay all over the floor like used newspaper. Pinky and Ira climbed in behind him.

"This ain't such a good idea," Ira said. "No telling what's in there."

"Then don't come," Pinky said.

She followed Leper on her tiptoes as he shuffled through the piles of paper money toward the darkness at the back of the store. Ira hesitated for a minute before catching up.

Leper whistled from the dark and the other two kids followed the sound of it until they found him standing next to a mechanical staircase with rubber banisters. The bottom steps of the staircase were barely visible in the dim light of the broken window up front. The steps led up into absolute blackness.

"What do you think it used to do?" Pinky asked. They were all born after the war.

Leper shrugged. Ira looked over his shoulder at the gray daylight shining through the broken window.

Leper started up the staircase. "Leper. Hey. What are you doing?" Pinky asked. "I can't see up there. It's too dark."

He held out a bandaged hand and tapped himself on the chest with the other, whistling through the hole in his mouth.

"You can see in the dark?"

He nodded.

"Cool."

She looked at his hand, hesitated. He whistled again, and Ira clutched at Pinky's free hand and followed. It was a mess up there, full of racks and heaps of old clothes. There were bodies, too. Leper was glad the other two kids couldn't see them. They were all folks who had died of the Miracle Plague in the dark, and that wasn't a very good combination for a couple of kids no matter how you put it.

Leper led them carefully around the bodies toward a patch of light that came from a very large window, much like the one on the bottom floor that Ira had smashed. "Look!" Pinky pointed.

Leper glanced at the corner of the room by the window and found something looking right back at him, something covered in rags and watching him with one bulbous bloodshot eye. He jumped back and wheezed in the back of his throat. The thing in front of him jumped back too and backed away into the darkness.

"Take it easy, Leper," Pinky said, grabbing him by the arm. She never was afraid to touch him. "Ain't you ever seen a mirror before?"

Leper touched himself on the chest and watched his arms go in the mirror. He touched the bandages on his face and he leaned in close to look himself in the eye. Then he stepped back and looked down at his raggedy cut-off jeans. He looked at the bandages that covered his legs and ankles and he wriggled the stump of his big toe through the hole in his shoe. He put his hands in his pockets and he stared for a long time. He had never seen himself before.

"Shit Christ Almighty!" Ira hollered. Leper looked past the mirror and found that Ira had found one of the bodies poking out of the shadows. Much of the leather skin had pulled back from the face to reveal red bone. It lay on its back but its back was bent – it had died in a lot of pain.

"That one died twice of the Plague," Pinky whispered. That meant that something had finally put it out of its misery. She went over to stand beside Ira and they both looked down at the body. Leper went back to looking at himself.

"That's bad," Ira said, stepping back toward the light of the window. "That's so bad. Get me out of here. I want to go."

"Just chill out," Pinky said. "It's not going to bite."

"How do you fucking know?" Ira started getting bent out of shape. "I want to get out of here. Get me out of here." He looked at Leper. "Take me back downstairs."

Leper looked at Pinky and back at Ira and took a step forward.

"Hang on a minute," Pinky said. "You want to go so bad and you never wanted to come up here in the first place. You want to go back now? Do it yourself."

"Well what the hell do you want to do up here?" Ira pushed up the bill of his ball cap so that Pinky could see his face. "You want to get worked on by your boyfriend here and all his relatives—"

Pinky's fat knuckles hit his jaw and he fell on his knees to the floor. Leper took a step back. He never liked fights. Pinky kicked Ira on the ass real hard and he fell on his face. His ball cap tumbled across the floor. He snatched it and scooted back from Pinky against the wall with his hand up in front of his face. His mouth was bleeding.

"You don't have to go be like them other bastards all the time, Ira," Pinky said. Leper couldn't take his eyes off of her. Her fat cheeks were burning so red that Leper wished he could put her face in a bottle and take it home.

"You could be a little nicer," Pinky snorted and waved her hand. "But if you ain't gonna be, get the fuck out of here. Find your own way home. I'm tired of protecting your weak ass all the time anyway."

Ira screamed back at her like a wounded animal and sprinted past the both of them into the dark, falling over racks of cloths and heaps of garbage. Leper watched him find the stairs with his hands and feel his way down them. He was sobbing out loud as he went back down.

"There's got to be something, you know?" Leper looked at Pinky, whose face still flashed bright red. She shuffled over to stand by the window and look out onto the street. "I ain't saying anything's going to save us. I know we're all going to die. But there has to be something."

Leper turned back to look at the mirror. An intact upright rack of clothes beside it caught his good eye.

"You and me are friends." Pinky was crying. "I'm tired of watching everything go to hell. I'm sorry I didn't step in for you yesterday. I feel real bad. Rosa Lee's a big girl, and you kind've had it coming."

Pinky turned around and found Leper staring back at her. He wore a wide-brimmed cowboy hat on his bandaged head that was way too big for him. He tilted it up with his thumb but it sank over his face down to his shoulders. She laughed so hard she had to bend over to catch a breath. Leper laughed too, the best he could at least. Pinky wiped her tears away and said, "What else they got?"

They tried on lots of clothes. Pinky found a long thick coat with fur on the collar. When she put it on and fastened the buttons it dragged behind her on the floor when she walked and you couldn't see her feet, like she was floating. Leper found a pair of pointy boots to go with the hat. The hat sat just right if he tipped it up to rest on the top of his forehead. The boots were too big and came up past his knees. They had hard soles—Leper jumped up and down in them and they made an awful racket against the floor. Every time he landed, the big hat fell over his face and Pinky snorted.

Pinky found a big long string of feathers. The colors, like everything else, were faded, and when she looked in the mirror and tossed her head high as she wrapped it around her neck, the feathers turned to dust and made her cough.

Leper knew that there were piles of bodies around them in the darkness. It was a big pack of folks infected with the Miracle Plague. They must have waited it out up there away from live folks and starved. Or maybe some live folks locked them in there. Either way, it was a long time ago.

He knew that Pinky couldn't see all of the bodies in the dark, and he made sure to keep quiet about it. For the first time, they had forgotten about the world and it had forgotten about them. For the first time in their lives, they played. And they did little else for the rest of the afternoon.

Somewhere inside Leper's half dead heart, hope grew like a green sapling.

~

When the ashen sky sunk into a deeper shade of grey, Leper took Pinky's hand and led her back down the mechanical staircase. They climbed over the threshold that used to hold the window Ira broke and walked down the street together toward the next intersection. There they would part ways. Pinky would go to where she lived with her momma and daddy beneath a freeway underpass and Leper would go back to Moo-ma, who should be finished with the strangers by now, and most likely worn out.

"Hey, freak," a voice growled from behind them. It was Rosa Lee.

Leper turned around but was met in the face by a rock the size of his fist. His feet flew out from under him and he landed on his back. Everything flashed bright before his eyes. He shook his head and got up on his hands and knees.

He looked up and saw big black Rosa Lee standing on top of the rubble pile with a stick in her hands. She had a crew of kids with her. They mostly hung around so she wouldn't give them a beating, which she did anyway sometimes, so it didn't really make any sense; but still they hung around.

Ira skulked behind Rosa's leg with his ball cap pulled down low over his eyes. His scrawny jaw had swelled so that it looked like he had bread in his mouth that he was saving to swallow.

"Ira!" Pinky hollered out. "What did you do?"

"Stay out of this, fat ass," Rosa Lee hollered back. She slid down the rubble pile with her posse tumbling behind her. Ira kept his distance.

Rosa stomped toward Leper like an angry bull. "You should never have been born. You a nasty, nasty son of a bitch." She smacked the stick against the flat of one hand. "Nobody touches my stuff. Especially you."

Pinky stood in front of Leper. "Get out of here, Rosa Lee," she said, her voice shaking. "Go on."

Rosa Lee kept coming and stuck her big black nose in Pinky's face. Leper heard tell that Rosa didn't have any folks and had to fend for herself for food and water. She didn't let any of the grown folk have their way with her either—she was just too damn big and tough.

Pinky folded her arms, though, and didn't budge. Rosa spat in her face.

Pinky's cheeks turned red. She took a swing at Rosa Lee. Her fist glanced off of the side of Rosa's jaw and forced her back a step. Rosa grabbed her by the wrist and brought the stick down on her head. Pinky fell to her knees. Rosa swung again. Pinky fell onto her face and didn't move.

Leper felt his cold blood begin to boil. He was mad that Rosa Lee hit Pinky. Rosa laughed. The other kids were quiet. Especially Ira, who stood on the pile of rubble with his hands shoved in his pockets.

Rosa came after Leper and swung the stick. It came down on his shoulder. She swung it again but he rolled out of the way and it cracked on the road. He jumped on her then and she fell back. He made a low sound in the back of his throat as he glared at Rosa's surprised face with his one good eye. He stuck his bandaged finger into her eye and she hollered, "Goddamn, get this kid off of me."

She fell on her back. Leper straddled her. The sound in his throat turned into a growl. He sat up straight and shoved a finger from each hand into the hole in his mouth. Rosa looked up at him, obviously terrified. He hooked both fingers and pulled.

Rosa Lee started screaming.

Leper howled as he pulled his lips apart through the black twine stitches, leaving the skin around his mouth in shreds. He dove forward for Rosa's face. She held her arm up in front of her. His rotten teeth sank into her forearm and he twisted and wrenched himself away, pulling a fat chunk of flesh away. Rosa stopped screaming.

Leper rolled off of her and chewed on the piece of skin, wringing it around in his mouth. He was something else now, the other half of himself. The dead half. The Daddy half.

Rosa sat frozen, looking at the glistening bone in her forearm. Blood mixed with black saliva dripped into her lap. "Oh," she said. "Oh."

Leper swallowed the last morsel of flesh and focused on Rosa again. She backed away from him and stood up. "Am I sick? Am I going to get sick?" She held her messed up arm away from the rest of her.

Leper opened his mouth to show Rosa his bloody teeth and took another step toward her.

Rosa Lee hollered and scrambled back up the rubble pile. Leper stared after her until she was out of sight. Then he stared at her gang. They held up their hands and backed off. In moments they were gone. Even Ira had scattered.

Pinky was still on the ground, but she was getting up. Leper bent over to help her up but she backed away. "Don't," she said.

He stopped and held out his hands. Leper felt better now. He was back to his old self. Pinky was having trouble figuring that out though, so he let her go without trying to talk her out of it. "Thanks," she mumbled as she backed away from him. "See you later." She was awful scared. He could see it in her eyes. The color in her cheeks had vanished. They were as pale and as ashen as everything else in the world.

Leper waited until she was out of sight before he began running. He ran through the alleys and the streets of the broken city, around the garbage and the excrement, through the fog and the ash toward home. He had done what Mooma had told him not to do. She said that it was very important that he keep his mouth shut. She said that he was a key to getting rid of the Miracle Plague for good, but that he also was the vehicle. Rosa Lee would surely get it—he didn't think of her as the big black girl who beat up everybody anymore. He felt sorry for her now. She would curl up and eventually die in some dark corner. Then she would come back. Everybody was going to be screwed all over again.

Leper stopped in front of his building and stumbled up the stairwell to the fifth floor. The door to their rooms was wide open. Inside, everything had been turned over and was scattered all across the floor. He looked in his room, expecting to find Moo-ma there, but she wasn't. She wasn't there at all. That wasn't like her.

He went through her things and found the roll of black twine and the needle. He took a fresh roll of bandages as well, and he brought all of these to his room. He sat down on the floor Indian style and looked out over the city's early evening fires. He sat the bandages and the twine down beside him and took out the cigar box from beneath the pile of rags that made his bed. He stopped thinking about the day and looked at all of the colors of the world while he waited for Moo-ma to come home.

**Jeremy Kelly** makes up stuff. He lives with his wife and kid in Decatur, Georgia. You can find him and some of his other stories at **jointhebirdies.blogspot.com**.

# The Outlaw Fringe
## A CONVERSATION WITH COUNT LYLE OF GHOULTOWN

by K. Allen Wood

Every so often an artist comes along and defines what makes something truly original, extraordinary. That something is sincerity. In the arts, few can lay claim to a patch of land all unto his or her own. With their unique slant on horror punk, Count Lyle and the band **Ghoultown** have done just that.

I was fortunate enough to catch up with Lyle—founder, frontman, and creative force behind the band—and discuss **Ghoultown's** past, future, and also his own forays into writing fiction and nonfiction under the name Lyle Blackburn.

If you've never heard of the band, you'll want to read on. And if you have, you'll want me to shut up.

I can dig that. Now dig this.

~

**KW: Let's talk about the days before Ghoultown, if you don't mind. You were the bassist in Solitude Aeturnus, one of the most beloved doom-metal bands in the world, before leaving the band in 1996, forming the horror-punk outfit The Killcreeps, and releasing *Destroy Earth,* the band's sole album. How do you make that stylistic jump? You also played with GG Allin, back in the mid 80s, and given that Ghoultown is musically closer to what you did with The Killcreeps, is punk more your style?**

**CL:** It's hard to narrow down my musical taste and influence into one single style. I'm really into 80s hardcore punk, and I sort of retain an overall punk attitude no matter what music I'm doing, but I also love dark stuff, metal and vintage country. Since I like so many different styles, it was hard to play in one kind of band for my whole musical career. That's probably why I ended up creating **Ghoultown.** It has elements of a lot of different styles and I'm able to keep myself entertained that way.

**KW: Solitude Aeturnus is still together, though fairly inactive, and The Killcreeps is no more. If you don't mind answering, why did you step away from those two bands?**

**CL:** I left **Solitude** for a few different reasons, none of them being that I don't get along with the other guys or anything like that. It was mostly because I felt I had done everything I wanted to with that particular style of music and also because I love to play live. With the type of metal **Solitude** plays, there is very little demand for it here in the United States like there is in Europe, so we didn't have the opportunity to play very many shows. Plus, after a while, I got bored with it. Doom metal is deep and introspective, which is cool, but after a while that's just not what I was into as a performer. I wanted to do something more upbeat and reckless like I used to do with my early punk bands. I guess I wanted something a little more crazy, and something that attracted a wider range of music fans, so I stepped away and started **The Killcreeps** in 1996.

I have always been a fan of **The Misfits**, so naturally I leaned toward horror punk. That's what my early punk bands like **The Holy** were. And the funny thing is that Robert Lowe, the vocalist for **Solitude**, played guitar for **The Holy**. So we both started off in a punk band. After that we had a metal band called **Graven Image** which sort of prepared us for joining **Solitude**.

I really love the *Destroy Earth* album I did with **The Killcreeps**, but in the process of doing that band, the **Ghoultown** concept was born. It was sort of like an evolution of self-expression for me. Once I started running with the idea of **Ghoultown**, I realized that it was the perfect way to express all my musical influences at once. It was also something that allowed me to work in my Texas roots, but still do something kind of dark. So it was a natural progression through some different styles until I reached something that was truly unique and something that I felt represented me best.

**KW: And of course the songs "Wicked Man" and "Rotoriculous" were later resurrected as Ghoultown songs. Any plans to reissue *Destroy Earth*?**

**CL:** I tried for years to get some other horror-punk label, like Fiendforce or whatever, to re-release the CD, but no one was ever interested—even though so many fans kept asking. And, oddly enough, **The Killcreeps'** track we put on Fiendforce's *This Is Horrorpunk* compilation got the best reviews, or at least in the reviews I saw. And it had been nearly a decade since the song was recorded, so that was kind of cool. But Fiendforce only wanted new material, which was hard to do since the project was no longer active.

I was trying to get away from releasing everything on my own label, so it just sort of sat on the shelf after the original pressing sold out. But good news, I just released a new digital-only remastered version through CD Baby (www.cdbaby.com/cd/killcreeps). Fans can download the whole album for a good price and also get the brand-new cover art by Jeff Gaither. The original cover wasn't great, so I thought that the new version should have a killer new cover.

**KW: Being from Texas, being exposed to the Old West in ways only living there can do, what inspires you to mix so many styles? Some influences are obvious: The Misfits, Johnny Cash. But what are some other influences? Any of the old country and western greats, like Bob Wills and Marty Robbins?**

**CL:** Growing up, my parents listened to a lot of vintage 60s and 70s country, so that was sort of ingrained in my brain at a very early age. My dad and I used to go hunting all the time around some of the small towns in south Texas, so if you wanted to listen to the radio, it was literally the only thing on. With the exception of a few artists like Johnny Cash, I pretty much hated that stuff when I was a kid, probably because it was what my parents liked. But as I got older, that music sort of crept back into my taste and eventually fused with my punk and metal styles... which ultimately resulted in **Ghoultown**. So yeah, I like pioneer country artists like Merle Haggard, David Allan Coe, Marty Robbins, George Jones, and all those great songwriters. But of course Nashville has killed country and western. It's sickening to hear what passes for country now.

As for the Old West, it definitely plays a big part in our music. The Old West was a rough and violent place and to me it fits nicely into the dark subjects I'm usually drawn to. I really love the Italian spaghetti westerns. They were not just cowboy movies...they were full of blood, swagger, and evil outlaws. I always wanted to grow up to be "The Bad" from *The Good, The Bad, and The Ugly*. I guess if you look at my **Ghoultown** image, I pretty much have...although I carry a Gibson guitar instead of Colt 45.

**KW: Despite mixing so many styles, it seems, from a fan's perspective, that Ghoultown is finding more and more success as time goes by. Obviously hard work and talent have a lot to do with this, but do you believe Ghoultown's rather unique brand of psychobilly cowgoth plays an equal—and possibly bigger—role in the band's popularity?**

**CL:** We do have a pretty good core audience, but I think the fact that **Ghoultown** doesn't fit neatly into one single music genre has limited our success quite a bit. We get crossover fans from psychobilly, but also from metal, punk, goth and whatever. But because we do not adhere to a strict style, for example straight psychobilly, we are not universally excepted by the majority of fans for any one kind of music... only the outlaw fringe. Same for horror punk, metal and whatever. So our fans are sort of renegades who don't feel like they have to stick to one certain scene or general music type. This is a challenge because we must win fans over one by one rather than just inherit a whole bunch of fans by default just because we play a popular style.

Over time I've come to realize that not fitting into a music genre of any type is a problem. We end up having to do everything on our own, creating our own brand of music and our own **Ghoultown** scene. It's also hurt our chances of ever getting picked up on a real tour. All of our tours have been us headlining. In 11 years we've never been able to score a tour as an opening act. Nobody seems to know what to do with us. It's great to headline, but except for a few one-off shows, we don't get the benefit of being in front of a big crowd night after night. A crowd of people that might not get exposed to us any other way. That's the fastest way for a new band to pick up fans. Everything we do is sort of on the fringes it seems.

**KW: Yeah, I understand that. I know Dean Koontz had a hard time early on because his novels mixed too many genres; they weren't just one thing, you know. Too many people need things black and white—black *or* white, rather; it can't be both. I remember when James Rivera couldn't get any promoter to book his band under the Distant Thunder name; they wanted Helstar. So he**

booked shows under that name—but it wasn't Helstar! Absurd.

**But let's say things weren't so ridiculous. What are some bands you'd like to open for, that you think would boost the band's popularity?**

**CL:** Yeah, we experienced the same thing James did while we were doing the **Maltoro** project. We were always billed as **Maltoro** aka **Ghoultown**. In the end, we should have just stuck with **Ghoultown** all along. We had already established a brand name with it, I guess.

As for bands to play with, we've always thought it would be great to tour with Hank III. We did one show with him and that went very well, so it's a pretty good combination. Maybe **Gogol Bordello** would be another good one. Beyond that, I don't know. Of course there are many smaller bands we could tour with, and have, but in this case I'm talking about doing a tour with an established band that draws a large crowd. Something that would expose us to more people at once.

**KW: You mentioned having to win fans over one by one. Though it may not be the ideal way to garner fans, and without thinking of the business side of things, do you think it's a bit more satisfying this way, when you know your hard work and art has touched each individual personally, rather than, say, a ton of people just jumped on a bandwagon because it's the cool thing to do?**

**CL:** Oh certainly, I would rather have the type of fans we have because they are all real, genuine fans of the music, not just followers. I probably wouldn't like it if all of a sudden there were people showing up just because they thought it was the cool thing to do. If I'm a fan of an underground band, I know I don't like it when all of a sudden the room is full of outsiders.

But in our case, where we have a solid but small following, I think it has limited our ability to realize the potential of **Ghoultown.** I have so many ideas about stage shows, videos, merchandise, and things like that, but at our level those things are usually not possible. I know I'm not the only artist suffering from this, but it doesn't stop me from thinking that if we just had some kind of boost then we could maybe play larger venues and make the whole **Ghoultown** experience better.

I'm probably biased, but I think **Ghoultown** is especially suitable for big shows. For example, I do an intro thing where I hang from a noose and get shot down. It's so cool, but hard to pull off in these small dives where we play. I wanted to build a free-standing rig that allowed me to do the hanging in any venue. But to drag that thing around would require a larger trailer or whatever, and that's just cost prohibitive at our level; and either way, we're usually lucky if we are on a stage that fits anything more than the six of us.

We've put everything we've ever made from this band back into it, so I guess I just regret that over the last eleven years we've not been able to implement all the cool things I originally envisioned for it. That leads to crazy ideas, like wanting more fans so we could really kick this thing into high gear.

**KW: I know some of the songs from *Bury Them Deep* were reworked versions of songs from the Maltoro project. Did any other songs end up on *Life After Sundown?***

CL: It's really mixed up. Some of the songs on *Bury Them Deep* were actually unrecorded **Ghoultown** songs that were used for **Maltoro,** then reverted back to **Ghoultown** songs. "Tekilla" and "Walking Through the Desert with a Crow" were both **Ghoultown** songs from the beginning. Everything on *Life After Sundown* was written solely for **Ghoultown** except "Werewolves on Wheels." That one was written during the **Maltoro** phase and then sort of re-worked to be more **Ghoultown**-ish. But the funny thing about most of the songs on *Life After Sundown,* is that they were written around 2003 to 2005 just after we did *Live from Texas.* So by the time those songs got recorded in 2008, they were already aged like a fine tequila. I like so many of the songs on that album, that I was relieved when we finally had a chance to record them.

**KW: The band's latest release, the limited edition CD/DVD *Mistress of the Dark,* features a new Elvira theme song of the same name. For those who haven't seen the DVD, would you mind talking a bit about how that song came to be?**

CL: We were playing an acoustic set at a horror convention VIP party where Elvira's manager happened to see us. He loved the band—even in our acoustic element—so he told Elvira (Cassandra) about us. The next day I was hanging out with some friends of mine at the convention and someone ran up and said, "Elvira wants to meet you, get to your booth." I thought it was a joke, but just in case I headed back to our booth where the **Ghoultown** girls had been selling t-shirts and CDs for us. Sure enough, Cassandra came by with her entourage and talked for a few minutes.

During that time she suggested I write a new song for her. I had a short meeting with her manager later on and came up with a plan to write a song and maybe shoot a video if it worked out. Two weeks later, I sent them a demo of the song, which they liked. From there we recorded it and decided to do a video. I called up our friend Gris Grimly out in Los Angeles and asked if he wanted to direct. He was excited about the opportunity, so once he was on board we headed out to Hollywood and shot the video. Cassandra was able to hook us up to use the Magic Castle out there, so that's where much of the video was shot.

The *Mistress of the Dark* DVD includes the video, a making of documentary, and some other crazy stuff that Grimly had us shoot. It's sort of like a bizarre take on an old 70s variety show. Like a horror version of the show *Hee Haw.* It's pretty crazy and campy, just like you would expect from Elivra. It was a cool experience.

*[Note: See the **Strange Goods and Other Oddities** section on page 52 for a review of*
*Mistress of the Dark.]*

**KW: Though a quintessential horror—and sex—symbol, do you think the younger generation of horror fans appreciate Elvira's iconic impact on the genre?**

CL: I think they do. Most people that are into horror seem to know who she is, even now. Her autograph line at the horror conventions is huge...people just keep coming by to see her. And now she has her new network television show that she launched this fall, *Elvira's Movie Macabre*. That should put her in front of even more new fans. So I think she will always be embraced by the horror crowd just as many of the past stars have.

**KW: You also worked with Gris Grimly a few years earlier by contributing the song "Ballad of Clarence Heckles" to the soundtrack of his short film *Cannibal Flesh Riot!* Think you'll work with him again in the future?**

CL: I hope so, but he's gotten pretty busy lately with some big-time projects. He's working as the art director for Guillermo del Toro's upcoming *Pinocchio* film. As a result of our Elvira project, he was asked to direct the intro for her new *Movie Macabre* show. Gris is such a cool guy and a talented artist and director, I'm glad he's getting to do such high-profile projects. He definitely deserves it.

**KW: A lot of Ghoultown's songs, particularly the lyrics, go a bit deeper than just dark; they tell stories. Do you ever foresee these songs being turned into films or fiction—short stories, novellas, etc?**

CL: I don't usually envision them as anything beyond just the song. Or at least I haven't yet. The only exception, sort of, is our song "Drink with the Living Dead." I'm working with an artist and a director right now to do an animated video for it. It's not total animation, but it uses artwork and some animation to tell the story of Stanton Cree from the lyrics. I don't have any idea yet of a release date for the video, but I can say that it's going to be really cool. I think it will be the next level for **Ghoultown,** having moved toward some type of animated characters. As I'm sure you can imagine, our style and image lends itself to that type of thing pretty easily. If this works out, maybe I can look into doing animated videos for some of the other story songs we have.

**KW: Speaking of stories, you write. You have a really cool blog over at the *Rue Morgue* website called *Monstro Bizarro,* where you discuss the legends and lore and other things surrounding some of the lesser-known but equally fascinating monsters that have appeared throughout history. You've also penned the stories for the Ghoultown comics, and I remember mention of you having written a novel as well, so what are your ambitions in terms of writing?**

CL: I've always been interested in writing and have done a few things in the past when time permitted. I recently started doing some writing for the great horror mag *Rue Morgue* under the name Lyle Blackburn. I've always been a huge fan of the magazine, and they've featured **Ghoultown** several times, so it's really cool to be working with them. It's kind of an interesting story as to how this came about.

As most of my friends know, I've always been into monsters—werewolves, vampires, zombies, and the usual sort—but also real-life monsters, so to speak, like bigfoot, yeti, sea serpents, chupacabra, all those type of cryptozoology creatures. I had some extra time, so I started reading some of the newer books on these creatures and decided to watch some of the bigfoot-related horror films out there that I hadn't seen. Of course, most of them totally suck, but there's some pretty entertaining ones if you search hard enough. This inspired me to write an article on the movies, which I ended up showing to Rod and Gary from *Rue Morgue*. They were down here for the Texas Frightmare Weekend horror convention, so we got a chance to hang out and talk. After discovering a mutual fascination with crypto creatures, we came up with the idea for my *Monstro Bizarro* column. So now I'm part of the blog staff on their website where I post about weird creatures or about upcoming movies involving cryptozoo monsters. I also write for the print magazine, covering the same type of subjects. I do movie reviews and I recently visited the International Cryptozoology Museum in Portland, Maine so I could do a write-up on that. It's in the new December issue of *Rue Morgue* (#107).

As fans know from the **Ghoultown** comic, I've been into writing off and on throughout my music career. I've always had a natural talent for it, and I have a Bachelor's degree in English, so it's something I've always been into. In some ways I feel like my lyrics are the best thing about my songs. So yeah, writing is something I like and I hope to do more of it in the future. I'm working on a nonfiction book right now.

**KW: About the Ghoultown comic, unfortunately only two out of four issues were published. Are there any plans to release those someday, maybe the whole thing as a graphic novel?**

**CL:** Those came out about ten years ago. What happened was, the publisher decided to stop doing comics right in the middle of the run. So only two of four issues of the mini-series came out. At the time, I submitted to all the other comic publishers to see if someone else wanted to pick it up and continue the series or re-release it. But I couldn't find anyone that was interested, or that could take on another title, so I just let it die.

It sucks that it left the readers hanging, but there wasn't much I could do about it. I was too busy running the label, writing songs, and doing band stuff that I just couldn't take on the task of comic-book production, too. It's very expensive to produce comics and almost impossible to get distribution in comic stores by yourself, so it was more of a labor-of-love situation and not a good business move to spend time on that when I had my hands full already with the music side of things.

At this point, I don't think those issues will ever be released in any format. Hell, I've still got boxes and boxes of the first two issues in my garage. I really don't have room for more.

**KW: And what of the novel? What's that about?**

CL: The **Ghoultown** novel was something I wrote back around the time of the comic book. It featured the same characters, so it was pretty much a book companion to the comic. I had an agent that shopped it around for years, trying to pick up a publisher, but again, nothing came of it. I think the novel is really good—even better than the comic—so I thought about self-publishing it, but I'm still reluctant to get into the publishing business.

My new book is nonfiction and has a much larger potential audience, so I don't think I'll have as much trouble finding a publisher for that. **Ghoultown** was considered horror-western fiction and that's just not something most publishers want to take a chance on. So as it stands, it's the best horror-western book that no one's ever read.

**KW: Back to *Monstro Bizarro*. Do you dig any of those shows like *MonsterQuest* and *Destination Truth?* Or do they irritate you as much as they irritate me? I mean, if you were hunting the elusive, never-been-discovered Bigfoot, would you be that goddamn *loud?* They might as well be a bunch of clowns riding through the woods on tricycles, honking horns and popping animal-balloons!**

CL: Ha. I hear ya. I do like *MonsterQuest* for the monster info and historical accounts, but the parts where they show researchers going out on expeditions or whatever are not very accurate. Like every other reality show, those parts are staged and scripted by the producers, so they are made to be entertaining, not scientifically accurate. Several friends of mine were featured on various *MonsterQuest* episodes, so they've told me stories about how those things went down. It's definitely not a good example of how you should go about hunting an animal of any kind. So yeah, real bigfoot researchers would not be so loud, nor would there be camera crews and producers around. But most of what goes on in a hunt for an undiscovered animal would end up as hours of boring footage on television, so I suppose they have to make it more exciting somehow.

I would rather see more of a documentary style approach where they just tell the history of the monster and talk about some of the cool reports. There's so many more credible sightings and stories that they never covered on *MonsterQuest*. Maybe I will launch a *Monstro Bizarro* show where I can do that.

After I get done with some of these other projects, that is. Ha!

**KW: So what lurks over the dusty horizon? What's next for the band?**

CL: The main thing now is to make some videos for some of our songs that never had videos. In the modern Internet age, it's important to offer something that can be viewed online to go with the music. We have some great songs, like

"Werewolves on Wheels," "Walkin' Through the Desert with a Crow," and of course, "Drink with the Living Dead," which never had videos.

**KW: So you're going to do videos for older songs? Obviously most bands focus on the current album, but it's not a bad idea to continue promoting older songs and albums, especially when they're strong. Which the older Ghoultown material is, of course.**

CL: I know that might seem strange, but I think we have some strong songs from the last two albums that really needed videos. If fans are putting the songs on YouTube themselves, with just the album cover sitting there as an image, I think that's saying something. I would rather have something cool that's done by us, at least for our most popular songs.

Fans always say that "Walking Through the Desert with a Crow" is one of their all-time favorites, so I regret that we couldn't make a video for it at the time. Doesn't mean that it shouldn't ever be done. Now we've met some really good video producers, so we have more of an ability to realize the potential of those great songs and perhaps expose them to more people by doing a video. We can't tour in every town in the world, but our video can be seen by anyone that has an Internet connection.

We have new fans joining the **Ghoultown** posse all the time, having just heard the band for the first time. They go back and buy all the past releases. I think that still makes those songs relevant. We're not going back beyond the last two full albums, so with the exception of "Walking Through the Desert with a Crow," the videos will all be from *Life After Sundown*.

**KW: Any timeline set for a new album?**

CL: I'm not sure when or if that is going to happen. As it stands right now, I haven't written any songs for it. Due to some personal things that have happened this past year, I haven't been able to find any **Ghoultown** inspiration. I sit down with the guitar all the time, but I can't seem to come up with a single riff. It's like a fire that has gone cold. I'm hoping that by going off and doing something totally different for awhile, like writing, it might reignite things, but at the moment I seem to be bone dry of musical ideas.

In the meantime, I've been thinking about releasing some sort of "rare and unreleased" type collection. We have so many old songs that never got released, or ones that were only on compilations or movie soundtracks, that it might be something cool for our long-time fans. We get e-mails asking about this track or that all the time, so I know some people would like to have our entire catalog. But at this point it's just an idea.

**KW: Well, I think we've all hit that wall at times, especially when personal issues come into play. Hopefully sinking your teeth into some other things will reignite that fire.**

**That said, the idea of rarities album has me excited. And who knows,**

maybe that'll be the spark you need and you'll pen a new Ghoultown song or two for the album. Either way, as a fan, a rarities disc would be killer.

**CL:** I did want to record a new song to include with the rarities album, so that's one thing that is holding it up. Once I get done with the latest video, I'm gonna try to work on this.

**KW: Anyway, brother, I appreciate you talking with me. Looking forward to whatever you do in the future.**

**CL:** You bet. Thanks for taking the time to support **Ghoultown.** And thanks for not asking questions like "Give me a brief history of the band." Our history is anything but brief. Ha!

For more information, visit **www.ghoultown.com.**

# Wanting It

by Aaron Polson

Megan doesn't ask where I go at night anymore. She knows. I'm sure she does. I hope she does. If she suspects something else—maybe an affair—I wouldn't want the hurt on my heart. Now that the kids are grown, it's just the two of us, and I've never loved—never *needed*—her more. But Megan can't take away the truth. She can't take away the nightmares, no matter how many times she squeezes my shoulder and whispers, "It's okay."

Nothing will ever be *okay*.

~

Joel and I started going to the pond in the sixth grade, two years before Robby moved to town. I was twelve and invincible: old enough to scoff at Santa Claus and the Easter Bunny, but young enough to let my imagination fill with the legends old men wrought as they sipped coffee at Daylight Donuts. *Haunted,* some would say. *A boy drowned there, back in the fifties. They dragged the pond but never found his body. His parents killed themselves right in the old farmhouse over the hill.* Invariably, a worn face would lean closer and whisper, *I heard he crawls out of the pond when folks go fishing up there, just to see who's troubling his water.* Joel and I listened, circling their broken, grizzled voices like summer moths.

We had been dreaming big dreams for years by then, dreams of ghosts and monsters and death. Sometimes, in our shitty little town, those dreams were all we had to avoid the real monsters of drunken parents and divorce. We had supped full of horror most of our childhoods, found escape with late night B-movies and old comics, *Creepy* and *Famous Monsters,* and as soon as we were old enough to win our parents' permission to ride our bikes alone, we made weekly trips to the pond and the old farmhouse.

But we never told them *where* we were going—never told them the truth.

We were the first to share the stories with Robby, and his gaping mouth and wide eyes said he was a kindred spirit.

"They say he comes out sometimes," Joel said, "to grab people when they're fishing."

I did my best to echo the old men. "Yeah. And the house—that's haunted, too. The kid's parents died there, and they've been looking for their boy for, like, forever."

Robby's face washed as white as the back of a postage stamp. "You guys ever see the dead boy?"

Joel and I exchanged a look.

"Not yet," Joel said.

~

I often dream of fishing at the pond with Joel. In the dream, our fishing tackle morphs into pulp comics with grotesque monsters on the covers and titles which include the words *Haunt, Fear,* and *Horror.* Joel looks up from one of the magazines, smiling. I dream until the dream bleeds to black, and I feel a giant's hand wrap around my heart and squeeze. Sweat stings my eyes as they open to my dark bedroom.

"What's wrong?" Megan asks.

"Nothing."

I lie. I can't tell her I choose the dream. Every night, I conjure the pond, the farmhouse, just before sleep—because a piece of me is always waiting there, wanting the impossible. I stare at the dark ceiling until Megan rolls over, her breathing slows, and she falls asleep. My clothes wait for me on the back porch. I've planned ahead. The drive out to the farmhouse takes only fifteen minutes, even in the dark.

~

We convinced Robby to come with us one weekend in early September of 1975. He didn't have his own fishing pole or bike. I loaned him my old Zebco 33, and Joel let him ride his Huffy while he stretched his ropey muscles on his father's ten-speed. We snaked along our usual path through Greenwillow Cemetery, rubber tires churning the gravel, a rough hum filling the space beyond the limestone gates.

We dropped the bikes and pressed under the loose barbed-wire fence at the back of the cemetery; Joel went first, I followed—each holding back the rusty links long enough for the other to step through—and Robby brought up the rear. Our imaginations spilled over into the shadows, bringing the breeze-blown tree branches to monstrous life. Robby's pale face turned at every sound, every snap of twig or brush of leaves.

When we ran out of bait, we hiked around the pond, past the overturned rowboat, and up over the rise. We stole into the old house through a loose door, opened Joel's backpack, and read his comics on the dusty floor until the shadows threatened our budding courage. We'd lived on the edge between adult *knowing* and childhood *believing* for two years. The stories those old men told at Daylight Donuts could have frozen our bones, but it didn't matter much to us. We wanted it. We wanted the dead boy to crawl out of the muck. We wanted the ghosts of his parents to whisper across our necks. We wanted it more than anything.

And we wanted Robby to feel the thrill, too.

He channeled our excitement that day—a sense of wonder which, for me, had become faded with time, just like the washed-out pages in Joel's comics. It was Robby who convinced Joel to take the boat out onto the water.

"It looks fine. It'll float just fine," he said. "Maybe we could see something out there. Maybe, if the water's still enough."

Joel looked at me. "Maybe."

"No," I said. "You guys are nuts." In my memory, I saw a rock leave Joel's hand, tumble through the sky, and strike the white plank hull. We'd dared each other to hit the boat with stones in the past, hoping to stir the dead boy from his muddy slumber. "That thing isn't going to float."

~

I park just outside the farmhouse. Inside, I stretch out on the floor, eyes pointed toward the ceiling. I lie there the remainder of the night. Uneven floorboards pinch my back, and my muscles stiffen by morning, but I don't move. I wonder who lived in the house. I think of the conversations which might have seeped into the walls and the stone foundation. What anger and love and sadness leaked into the plumbing and the shards of glass strewn across the floor. The old house seems to breathe.

But it's only the wind.

The moan of the old wood.

No voices come, no phantoms. Only daylight and a trip home.

~

I watched from the opposite bank as Robby and Joel turned the boat over. Joel kicked it, testing its integrity. They heaved it into the water.

"Hey, Talbot! It floats!" Joel flipped me off from across the water. "Floats just fine, chicken shit!"

It floated fine until they paddled to the center of the pond, using their cupped hands as oars. Robby stood up, and the boat teetered. Joel tugged at his jacket, but Robby didn't sit down. My legs wobbled as though I were standing in the rocking boat with them. They capsized, dropping into the water with a thunderous splash and spray of water.

I closed my eyes, trying to see a boy, all alone, fall in the water twenty-five years before and drown. I tried to conjure his spirit, invite him to join us as my friends thrashed against the chilly water. I begged for it.

"Help us," Joel cried out.

I opened my eyes and waded into the pond past my waist. Water and mud bled together, obscuring the bottom. The murk encircled my legs, cradled my butt and testicles, and swallowed my shoes. I struggled against the pond as if it were a living thing. But then, as I reached Joel and Robby and found myself in water up to my chest, I realized it wasn't alive. It was dead, not even deep enough to swallow a body and never give it up. I thought of old men and their lies, and a glimmer of childhood wonder sank to the bottom with the mud. Grabbing each other's hands, we staggered to the pond's edge.

"Damn," I said, panting on the shore.

Robby looked at me. "Be real easy to die out here. Bet that's what happened to that kid."

Doubt sank its sharp claws into my thoughts. I looked at the pond, at Joel and Robby, both drenched and reeking of decaying pond matter, and at the little boat which managed to drift across to the opposite shore after capsizing. Even the words "opposite shore" now seemed like a lie. The pond was tiny, not much more than a drainage ditch in an old field. I felt cold, the same awful, empty sensation that gripped me after I saw Mom sneak Christmas gifts under the tree when I was seven. The same hollowness I felt when I caught Dad with Mrs. Reed at the park before the divorce. If there ever was a time for the dead boy to rise…

But he didn't. He never had, and he never would.

"There's no kid," I said.

Joel's surprised face turned up toward mine.

"But you said…the pond was haunted. Everybody knows." Robby held out a hand like a beggar hoping for a coin. "Everybody in town knows."

"Just stories," I muttered. "Just old men and their bullshit."

Wading into that pond, I'd peeked behind the curtain of those old men's stories, and seen the truth. The knowledge hollowed out my guts, made me an empty shell, a cold, numb bag of skin and bones.

In a way, I was the first to die.

~

The adult me knows what the child never wanted.

There's no body in the pond. No ghosts in the old farmhouse. I lie on the hardwood floor and wait all night, sometimes sleeping, sometimes awake. At dawn, it's Megan's face I think of, and I drive home.

We don't speak of the house anymore. She's happy I bought the place; happy I might finally put the past behind me.

But some memories have teeth, and they bite deep.

~

On Halloween night, Joel and I would watch old movies on *Varney the Vampyre's Horror Emporium,* a local cable rip-off of Morgus and Elvira. We thrilled to Boris Karloff in heavy spirit-gum and Bela Lugosi with his accent, thick like the mud at the bottom of the pond. Robby was going to join us at Joel's house our eighth-grade year.

We huddled in Joel's basement with bowls of buttery popcorn and nachos. We were both wired from cans of soda, caffeine humming through our veins—a sure guarantee we wouldn't nod off until the third film of the evening. The title credits for *The Black Cat* flickered on screen, both of our vintage horror heroes with starring roles.

"When do you suppose Robby's going to get here?" he asked.

"He'll come," I said.

Light from the television danced in Joel's eyes like stars on the dappled surface of a pond at midnight. Neither of us spoke for a time, both all too aware of the mutual unease which grew in our chests like hidden mushrooms in the spring.

We remembered the argument from school, the dare which played out between Robby and me.

On the TV, Lugosi raised a scalpel in one hand, ready to exact revenge on his nemesis, when the phone rang.

"Joel," his mother called from the top of the stairs. "Telephone."

The fungus burst in my chest, and its poisoned spores found my voice. "It's Robby's mom," I said. "Something's happened."

The look on Joel's face seared into my brain—the way his mouth dangled open and the shadows blacked out his eyes like pits pressed into black soil. He would have the same look four years later at the football stadium, hours before he would hang himself. "Bullshit," he muttered. "Bullshit."

But it wasn't bullshit. Robby took my dare, he took the challenge.

"If the pond's haunted," I'd said earlier in the week, "then prove it."

Robby's face brightened, and he said, "I'll go at night."

"Not alone you won't," Joel said. "That's a stupid idea."

"Check out the farmhouse, too. Nobody lives there anymore."

Robby smiled with narrow eyes. "Halloween night."

The phone call *was* Robby's mother. She was looking for him, of course. Joel and I knew where he was. Thought we knew, anyway; we tried hard to convince ourselves it wasn't true. The Sheriff's department pulled his body out before dawn, fat and bloated, like a worm on the sidewalk during April rains. There was a taint of blue to his skin, the cold blue of death, of stone, of the grave. Robby almost had a smile on his lips.

His mom moved away the next week, taking Robby's body with her. He had only been ours for a few months and he vanished like smoke.

Four years passed. Joel grew out of his old skin and found a new one, thick as leather and swollen with broad shoulders and heavy muscles. I always imagined the knuckles of his father's whiskey-soaked fist toughened him for football. He received scholarship offers in the mail. He signed with Kansas State. We didn't talk about Robby anymore, and we had watched *Varney* for the last time on that long-ago Halloween. After Robby's death, the exact ownership of the pond and surrounding property was disputed in local court, but the deeds of neither land nor house were ever found. The county took possession and erected stouter fences, put up NO TRESPASSING signs. Our Friday afternoon trips became distant memories. Joel's mom even threw out the comics.

Megan moved to town during our junior year. She was tall and lovely, with soft, natural tumbles of brown hair. Hazel eyes which you could reach into—push your whole body into and never find the bottom. Joel and I both chased her, nearly flaming out in our idiocy; in the end, she chose GPA over all-league linebacker.

The last time I heard Joel's voice, she was there, holding my hand.

"Hell of a game," I said. "Three sacks, interception—you'll go pro someday, and I'll beg for a loan. Just wait."

Joel shook his head. His water-slick hair glistened under the stadium lights. "You two going to the dance?"

"Of course. See you there, right?"

"Right."

Megan tugged my hand toward the car, but I resisted. There was something else on Joel's mind, some of which swam just behind his eyes.

"I went out to the pond after practice the other night," he said.

"The pond?"

"You can sneak in real easily if you drive around by the house—the old house where we hung out back in junior high. Remember?"

I nodded. Megan squeezed my hand.

"Just—it was really peaceful." He glanced at the ground and then let his eyes find mine. "Quiet, too. Nothing stirring."

I nodded.

Megan and I left Joel standing there, blank-faced under the lights, and expected to see him later at the dance.

We spent the rest of the night lost under the DJ's influence, spinning around the cafeteria turned dancehall. We snuck away, found a dark hallway, and slipped our tongues into each other's mouths, hands groping and searching our bodies in the dark near the school woodshop. Joel forgotten.

He hanged himself later that night. Megan wasn't the reason why; it wasn't our little game of chase which led to Joel standing on an old stool in the abandoned farmhouse. It wasn't jealousy which squeezed the life from his body, slowly, as the noose pressed the carotid arteries and the walls of his windpipe together, the rough strands of rope burning into his well-muscled neck.

No. Joel *wanted it.*

Joel wanted it as much as Robby did. He wanted ghosts. He wanted the pond to hold the silver-screen phantoms of Lugosi and Karloff, the monsters and ghouls from copies of *Tales from the Crypt* and *Haunt of Fear* we'd read into the late afternoon, sitting under shafts of light in the derelict house. Joel left all his want swaying there with his body—and maybe, just maybe, he'd hoped he could leave a lingering ghost for his old friend. He'd gone out a few days before his death, hoping to hear from Robby, wanting something bigger than any of us, but not finding it. That's what he meant by *quiet.*

~

Joel did it for me more than anything, and I knew it. I felt it in my blood when they lowered his casket into the earth at Greenwillow, burying him less than half a mile from the pond and the farmhouse where he'd died. Maybe he thought he had given me what we always wanted when we spent hours talking about ghosts and ghouls and things which lived beyond our knowing, not realizing the real fear came from recognizing those monsters didn't wait for us at all.

But I know. I've known ever since the day Joel and Robby tipped the boat into the water. Since the day I helped pull them out and realized the pond was nothing but a dirty ditch in a forgotten field. Nothing special. Nothing mysterious. That day, peeking behind the curtain, I saw old men telling stories to thrill a couple of stupid kids.

A whole legion of gaunt specters could rise from the cold, still waters of that pond and it wouldn't change what I know now—it wouldn't change the way I tremble in the dark, wishing for something I won't ever have back, yearning for one word, one whisper, when all the world has left for me is silence and the cold oblivion of the grave.

No ghost has ever crawled out of the pond. There's never been a spirit in the old farmhouse. I've looked. I've wasted my life trying to make something of Robby's drowning and Joel's suicide. I've listened for both of my friends in the dark, lonesome hours of the night. I've cried their names in my dreams, asking them for just a little sign—something, *anything*—that might take me back to that twelve-year-old boy who believed.

**Aaron Polson** lives in Lawrence, Kansas with his wife, two sons, and a tattooed rabbit. Several new stories are forthcoming in *Shimmer, Midnight Echo, Space* and *Time,* and other publications. *Loathsome, Dark and Deep,* a novel of historical horror is available from **Belfire Press.**

You can visit Aaron on the web at **aaronpolson.blogspot.com.**

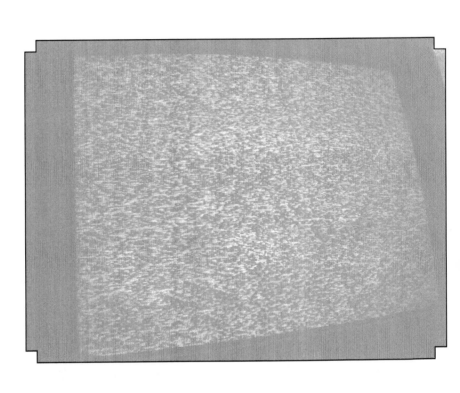

# Eye, You

by Joseph Morgado

You are in the living room of your dimly-lit apartment, lying on the Tylösand sofa from Ikea that your parents bought you when you first moved in. Your iBook laptop is propped open on your stomach, your hands interlaced behind your head, your head on a pillow. Your battery is charged, your Wi-Fi signal is strong—you are wired.

You've updated your Facebook page with details about the Stasi Fems gig you went to last night at Euclid's. You've posted the video you shot on YouTube.

Now you're watching a live webcam stream of Harmony, who recently joined your UIC Alumni Network and friended you, making her the newest of your 1,984 friends. She's wrapped in a bathrobe and sitting on the edge of her bed. She stands and drops her robe to the floor. You watch as she artfully moves her hands over her thighs, your face glowing in the glare of the laptop screen. Her hands slowly creep upward, over her stomach, and abruptly stop. You squint, waiting for more, but she remains frozen.

Your cat is playing with the power cord of the Wi-Fi modem—you have been unwired.

Sighing, you close the laptop, admiring the Apple logo on the lid that differentiates you from the *hoi polloi*. You consider getting up and plugging the modem back in so you can continue with Harmony, or maybe post some stills from last night's gig on Flickr. Instead you place the laptop on the Markör pine coffee table you bought to match the sofa. You clasp your hands behind your head and close your eyes.

Your iPhone buzzes. It's Oskar.

No, you're not going to Archimedes tonight. No, it doesn't matter that Daisy will be there. It's Friday, eviction night. Yes, you really can watch reality TV. No, you don't think you're partaking of the dregs of entertainment or the exploitation of the lowest common denominator. You offer the Warholian cliché about fame. Oskar offers a final caveat about Daisy, then hangs up.

### * *video disruption* *

You're sitting on the sofa, your feet kicked up on the coffee table next to four empty Corona bottles. You hold a fifth, half-full, as you watch *Big Brother*. The housemates are crying as they say farewell to their evicted colleague, the one they nominated because of her general lack of hygiene, congeniality, and class. She also ate all the shrimp. You Tweet your impressions of the girl's eating habits from your phone. The inquisitive followers of your Twitter feed will find it amusing.

The credits roll over a room full of sulking housemates, some hugging, one stroking the head of a girl weeping uncontrollably. You turn off the television and lie down on the sofa. You decide to post those stills of last night's Stasi Fems gig on Flickr, but you need a change of scenery. You get up and walk into the bedroom.

You sit down at your desktop iMac and plug in your camcorder. You download the footage and isolate some stills. You launch Internet Explorer, but before going to Flickr you check your Facebook page to see if Harmony has posted anything on your Wall. It takes a bit longer than usual to load, and when it finally does you're puzzled. You check the URL. You refresh the page a couple of times. You're still puzzled. It's not Facebook—it's live streaming video of you, sitting at your desk in front of your computer. You move your face close to the screen, trying to make sense out of what you're looking at. Indeed, it's you—same faded jeans, same *Miskatonic University* t-shirt, same red socks. You see yourself at different angles, in wide views and close ups: a profile from the side; your hand on the mouse; an aerial shot from the top; the freckle on your right earlobe.

The source of the live video might be the camcorder, you think, even though it couldn't provide the constantly changing views you see of yourself. You unplug it, but the video remains on the screen. You stand up, wave your arms, hop up and down. It's definitely you, live at that very moment, you are sure.

There must be a source somewhere, so you walk the perimeter of the room and examine the walls. You remove the picture of the Chicago skyline that hangs above the bed. There's nothing behind it but a nail. The live video shows the wall without the picture, then a close-up of the nail.

You climb up on the bed and examine the ceiling. You note that it was a wise decision not to cover it with mirrors, as Cassandra had suggested. You randomly rap it with your knuckles, but there's nothing unusual. The ceiling is solid.

Your phone goes off and interrupts your investigation. You answer, and hear a familiar angry voice on the other end. Shit. You've had this conversation with Libby before. Twice. Yes, you are sorry. Yes, you filmed it without her knowing and you regret it. Yes, you posted it on your Facebook page when you were drunk and friends have seen it, perhaps along with thousands of strangers. Yes, you were stupid for not restricting public access to your page. Of course you know all this, but you were drunk when you did it and at least the censors took it down. No, you didn't know her family had heard about it, and now she has to deal with all that shit. Yes, you admit that it was a stupid thing to do and you had no right. She hangs up on you.

You sit back down in front of the computer and watch yourself watching yourself. You find this all very perplexing, and wonder if you've had too much to drink. Five Coronas? Maybe you're becoming a lightweight. You lean back in the chair and look up at the ceiling as you stretch, noticing the light fixture mounted to the oak crossbeam of the A-frame. You grab a screwdriver from the desk drawer, climb onto the chair and fiddle with the fixture. You carefully remove the screws. As you probe around the wires, you jam the screwdriver in too far and short out the fuse. The electricity goes out, leaving you in darkness.

You yell out a compound expletive.

It's morning and you're casually leaning against a wall in the bedroom with a hammer in your hand. The curtains are drawn and the room is flooded with light. You've been working at it for a couple of hours now and the room is a wreck. There are jagged holes knocked into the ceiling and walls that reveal nothing but pink insulation and bare red brick. The light fixture dangles from its wires, plaster and debris scattered around the floor. You've replaced the blown fuse and the computer is on. You stare at the live video of yourself on what is supposed to be your Facebook page, leaning against the wall in the ruins of your bedroom.

Your phone buzzes. It's Oskar. You sit down and watch yourself while he fills you in on the events of the previous night. Yes, it's great that Daisy was asking about you, but you really want him to check your Facebook page. You can hear Oskar typing on his keyboard. Wow, he says, who's Harmony? Oh, and he's got to tell you what Daisy said about you. You cut him off and ask him what he sees. It's your Facebook page. Anything else? There's a very naughty message posted on your Wall, and why haven't you told him about this Harmony? Oh, and you're going to Pythagoras with him tonight at nine, no ifs, ands, or buts. There's a band playing that he really wants to see. He says he'll come by to pick you up at nine, then hangs up.

The phone goes dead as you stare at the screen, watching yourself watch yourself.

### *video disruption*

Oskar's standing in the doorway to your bedroom, his mouth open, eyeing the damaged walls and ceiling. No, your slumlord has not seen this. You tell him to come in and look at the video on your Facebook page. Look, it's you, live. Oskar walks over and sees you on the screen, sitting at your desk in front of the computer. Very nice, he says, but it's time to go get a drink. You're not in the mood for a drink. Doesn't he get it? That's you, right then, right there. It's some kind of… you don't know… but look at it, it's you, live. Oskar says it's obviously a recording you made—if it were live he'd be in it, too. You're shocked, and not because Oskar has made an impressive observation, which is usually out of character for him. He is most definitely not in the video. You look at Oskar, standing right beside you. You look back at the screen, but he's not there—it's just you.

You decide you could use that drink after all.

### *video disruption*

Pythagoras is packed and you were lucky to get a table close to the stage. The Georgie Whorewells are playing a cover of AC/DC's "Shoot to Thrill." Not bad for a chick band, you think, but you're not paying that much attention. You are preoccupied.

Before Oskar came over you called up Jamalay and Heloise and asked them to check out your Facebook page. When they did, both asked who Harmony was, but they saw nothing unusual. It seems this live video does not exist outside of your own web browser. You are disconcerted. Someone has to be playing a joke. Someone must have sent you a malicious virus in an email. Libby? Not technologically savvy. There must be a rational explanation for this. Yes, it has to be a disgruntled ex. Posey? Now there's a woman scorned. Maybe Helena? She was pissed when you broke it off. Well, you were never really together in the first place; that was just her perception of things.

You finish your second pint of Guinness and feel a little less anxious, a little more warm and fuzzy. You pull out your phone to Tweet about how much you love Guinness, but Oskar grabs it and stuffs it into his pocket. Give it a rest, he says. You turn your attention back to the Whorewells. They're sounding better with every song, looking better, too. Especially the bass player, whom you're ogling with extreme prejudice. And you're sure the Guinness is not doing the listening and looking—not yet, anyway. Oskar is absorbed in the band and nodding his head to the music. He loves chick bands and is on another planet. You ask if he's ready for another round, but there's no answer. You'll just get him a Stella.

The crowd is thick and difficult to navigate, but you finally reach the bar. Melanie is at the helm tonight and you make small talk as she draws the taps. You're wondering why you've never hit on her when you notice the security cameras on the wall behind the bar, swiveling on their mounts and capturing the action around the room. You give Mel a twenty and she goes to get change. You begin to feel uneasy. You look up at the cameras again and find that they've stilled and are pointing directly at you. Fingers snapping in your face interrupt the moment and Mel gives you your change. When you look back at the cameras they are swiveling again, scanning the room. You go back to your table and set down the pints. Oskar's enthralled with the music and doesn't notice.

## * video disruption *

You're in the bathroom at the sinks, splashing water on your face. You dry off, take a deep breath and exhale. You casually look around, making eye contact with a couple of other people washing their hands. You notice the single security camera mounted above the hand dryer. It's pointing directly at you. You try to ignore it, thinking perhaps it's not the swiveling kind, but you begin to feel uneasy again. You duck into a stall and lock the door. You go through the routine, you flush. As you're about to unbolt the door you hesitate. You peek over the top at the camera—it's pointing directly at you. You get a metallic taste in your mouth. You burst out of the stall, startling the others, and rush out the door. They notice that you didn't wash your hands.

You weave through the crowd and arrive back at the table to find that Oskar has ordered another round of pints and shots. You immediately down the shot.

The Whorewells are on break so Oskar is more aware of what's going on around him. He asks if you're okay, you look a little frazzled. Did Melanie shoot you down? You really should have gone with them last night because Daisy was very drunk and telling him all kinds of things she'd like to do to you.

Oskar's lips are moving, obvious that he is speaking, but you can't pick the words out of the sounds coming from his mouth. You grab your pint of Guinness and drink it down, without pause.

*\* video disruption \**

Your elbows compete for space with the empty glasses on the table. You haven't said anything coherent for a while. You're not sure about Oskar but the odds are against it. You get up uneasily and tell him you need some air. The Whorewells are back on stage playing another AC/DC cover—"Giving the Dog a Bone"—and Oskar is intensely nodding his head. He doesn't notice when you leave the table.

*\* video disruption \**

You walk down the street, breathing in the cool night air. Your head clears a bit and moves closer to its normal mode of thought. Maybe when you get back to the bar you'll chat up the Whorewells' bass player after the gig. You liked the cut of her jib, among other things. You smile. You walk past the Hancock building. High up towards the top a single, round office window is lit bright white. A black dot of a figure peers out through its center, looking out at the city. Someone is working late.

After a few minutes you see the sign for Chi-Town Video. There's a reason you don't like to go in this shop—namely Matilda, and she's working tonight. They also never have *Chasing Amy* in stock and you've wanted to see it for a while. Still, you go in to check and the bell on the door rings. Matilda looks out from behind a stack of DVDs on the counter and waves all too enthusiastically.

There are a few late-nighters milling around the racks as you browse. One is a cute strawberry blonde with freckles. You have a thing for freckles. Other than her, you don't see anything that catches your eye. Of course *Chasing Amy* isn't there. *Ghost World* is playing on the televisions hanging from the ceiling but you've seen it. You walk to the counter and ask Matilda if anyone has returned a copy of *Chasing Amy* that hasn't been re-racked. She says she'll check and walks over to a large bin filled with DVDs. She begins to rummage through them and cheerily mentions that *Clerks* is a better Kevin Smith film. You've seen it.

The strawberry blonde walks up to the counter with two DVDs and quietly queues behind you. You're trying to think of a clever opening line when Matilda asks why you haven't called. You knew this was coming. You're just about to tell her to forget it and go back to the bar when the strawberry blonde asks what film you're looking for. You turn to answer with a smile. The smile quickly fades. You notice that the televisions hanging from the ceiling are no longer playing *Ghost*

*World*—they're playing live video of you, standing at the checkout desk in Chi-Town Video. The metallic taste returns to your mouth. The video on the televisions simultaneously cuts to close-ups of your trembling hands, your eyebrow ring, the red socks peeking out between your jeans and Sambas. The video changes to a wider shot, but the strawberry blonde isn't standing next to you, and Matilda is not rummaging through the bin of DVDs behind the counter. The video shows only you, standing alone in Chi-Town Video.

You scream and run out of the store.

A bewildered Matilda returns to the counter, a copy of *Chasing Amy* in her hand. The strawberry blonde shrugs and says she'll take it.

### * *video disruption* *

You burst into your apartment and slam the door, locking and chaining it. You're breathless, but sober now. You stumble to the sofa and sit down, resting your head in your hands. After your breathing slows you hear a gauzy hum coming from the bedroom. You didn't shut down the computer before you left.

You walk into the bedroom. You stare at the millions of stars coming towards you on the screensaver. Even as you wonder what's on the other side, what a nudge of the mouse will reveal, your hand is already there, the star field evaporates and there you are—a wide shot of you in the room cuts to close-ups of the damp strands of hair on your forehead, then the tiny cleft in your chin.

You close your eyes, hard, and have an idea. You walk into the closet, dig around for a few moments and emerge with your cricket bat. You casually walk back to the desk and make short work of the computer, which explodes in a shower of sparks. You move on to the keyboard, mouse, and speakers. Mission accomplished. You sit on the floor among the debris and take off your Sambas. They laughed at you when you joined the cricket team at UIC. Who's laughing now? You'd like to Tweet about your vindication, but Oskar's got your phone. You get up and walk out of the bedroom.

### * *video disruption* *

You are in the living room of your dimly-lit apartment, lying on the Tylösand sofa from Ikea that your parents bought you when you first moved in. Your iBook is propped open on your stomach. Your battery is charged, your Wi-Fi signal is strong—you are wired.

You launch Internet Explorer, but forget about that Tweet because you need to update your Facebook page with the details about your night out with Oskar. You also need to add the Georgie Whorewells to your list of likes, join the *I Love Guinness* group and check out what Harmony has posted on your Wall, maybe even pick up where you left off with her in that web cam session. You select Facebook from your bookmarks and wait for the page to load. It takes a bit longer than usual, but when it finally does you giggle. You check the URL. You refresh the page a couple of times but it still shows the same live video—you, lying on your sofa, watching yourself. You smile as the video cycles through episodes of your past. You see yourself newly born and in your mother's arms; at seven in the boat with your father on Lake Michigan; at fifteen telling your parents that you are gay; at eighteen running through the vineyards of Bordeaux with Daphne; at twenty-two in your cap and gown; skiing in New Zealand with Mandy last September; two weeks ago in the bedroom of Libby's apartment, kissing her neck, whispering that no one will ever know; writing code in your cubicle on Friday afternoon; drinking with Oskar at Pythagoras; staring at the strawberry blonde in Chi-Town Video; lying on your sofa, watching yourself watch yourself. Ah, memories, you think. You shake your head and giggle.

You get up and walk into the bedroom, leaving the open laptop on the Markör pine coffee table you bought to match the sofa. The live video on the laptop screen shows you rummaging in the closet. You emerge with the bungee cord that tied your skis together. You grab the desk chair and position it beneath the A-frame in the ceiling. There are close-ups of the mascara streaking down your face, the mood ring—a gift from Libby—on your middle finger, the sweat stain under the collar of your *Jesus Cthulhu Superstar* t-shirt. You climb onto the chair and wrap one end of the bungee cord around the oak cross beam, the other around your neck.

You step off the chair. There's a shot of your legs kicking in the air, then swinging, then twirling. And then all movement abruptly stops. Your red socks halt at the edge of the screen and remain frozen.

Your cat is playing with the power cord of the Wi-Fi modem—you have been unwired.

**Joseph Morgado** lives in Cornwall in the United Kingdom, where he teaches literature, surfs, and grows raspberries and pumpkins. He is working on his first book of short fiction.

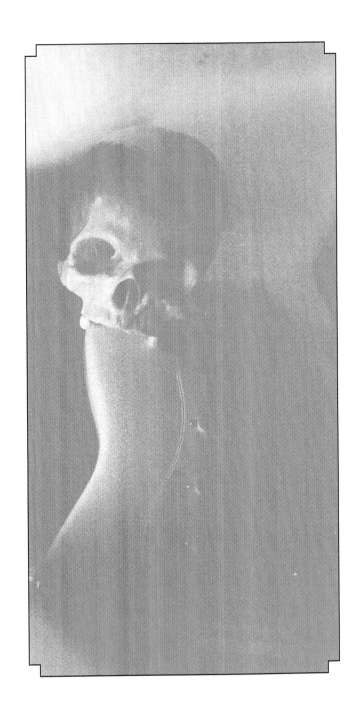

# Bloodstains & Blue Suede Shoes

by John Boden and Simon Marshall-Jones

## PART I: THE AIM

Horror and music have had a tight relationship for centuries, as far back as medieval times, when minstrels would sing of witches and evil kings and murderous things. Childhood staples like "Ring Around the Rosie," so sweet and innocent from the mouths of babes, but in fact a song about the horrors of the Black Plague. There are numerous grisly operas and quite a few classical works based on dark themes. And then we have all manner of murder ballads and dark blues, and that track runs on to the current offending styles of death metal, grindcore, gothic, darkwave, industrial, and countless other genres and splinter groups. All are the slobbering mutant progeny of music and horror—monstrous parents who pinch their young and pull scary faces at them in the dark before bedtime.

In this series, we hope to explore as many of these offspring as we can. We will try by genre and artist to enlighten, educate, and expose you to musicians and their hymns to the darker side of existence; artists both well-known and obscure. As well, we'll be exploring what we feel tethers them to the starless abyss.

We will no doubt cover most of the more high-profile offenders: **Alice Cooper, Rob Zombie, Nick Cave** (with and without the **Bad Seeds**), **Blue Oyster Cult, Wednesday 13, Misfits,** and **Ghoultown,** to name just a few. We also plan to cover a lot of unfamiliar ground, those artists and songs that don't always spring to mind when you think of a horror-themed song. Take, for example, Josh Ritter's "The Curse," a hauntingly beautiful ballad about a Mummy and his ill-fated affair with the archaeologist who discovers him. Or take the fad for teen-death/tragedy pop songs of the ghoulish '50s and '60s, like "Tell Laura I Love Her," a chart-topper for Ray Peterson in 1958, or the **Shangri-La** hit from 1964, "Leader of the Pack." It's a long, dark, and bumpy road we'll be traveling, one snaking with curves and blind spots.

From Robert Johnson and his supposed satanic connections to **Led Zeppelin's** and the **Rolling Stones'** apparent witchery. From the Buddy Holly curse of 23 and the murderous evils of black metal—which is still causing our moral guardians to froth rabidly at the mouth—to the more recent rumblings of dark ambient, neo-folk, and the bludgeoning noise and power electronics of death industrial. We shall journey thence to the gothic strains of **Bauhaus,** to the classicism of Hector Berlioz and the howling psychobilly of **The Cramps,** to the oddball novelty of **Barnes & Barnes** and **The Residents,** and on to corpse-paint and glitter rock. We will eventually haul it all in, across the bloodstained carpet and onto the ceremonial slab, slice it open, spread its ribs, and have a good poke around to see what hides in the dark depths of its insides.

For me—John, that is—the initial example of the unholy union between music and horror begins and ends with Alice Cooper. There were theatrics in music before he came along—Jerry Lee Lewis had set his piano on fire; "Screaming" Jay Hawkins worked the voodoo angle—but no one did it with the bloodcurdling gusto of The Coop. His albums were concept works, built around themes of giant spiders, necrophilia, murder and madness. Even something like a trip to the dentist was nightmarish when rendered by Cooper and his band. I was, maybe, five years old when I first became aware of Alice. My parents were fans and played *Welcome to My Nightmare* quite often. According to them, I was very fond of the song "Steven."

Cooper used to appear on television, and I recall sort of mini-movie versions of his songs. I seem to remember a disturbingly creepy video for "Dead Babies," which ends with Cooper being lynched. Though this may be something I made up, I can't be sure. Hell, he was on *The Muppet Show!*

Anyway, it started with him. I was already into all manner of horror films by the time I could walk, and as I began to become conscious of music and "older" tastes, I sought out things that were dark and horror-related. I liked looking through my parents' stacks of albums. The cover for **Steppenwolf's** *Monster* sticks out as one I went to often. After Cooper, I got into **Kiss.** Not quite as dark musically, but that look—goddamn! I wanted to *be* Gene Simmons! And there were others, including **Blue Oyster Cult,** a fantastic band we will no doubt devote some more space to in the future.

By the time I hit my teens, I was in love with music, rabidly so. I was obsessed with it. I was into things my mother listened to—Tom Petty, John Stewart, Meat Loaf, **The Eagles,** Jackson Browne—and was getting into the heavy-metal scene with acts like **Iron Maiden, Lizzy Borden, Dio** and **The Plasmatics.** By my short-lived college days, I had broadened my tastes to include alternative styles and artists like **The Smiths, Bauhaus, Pixies, The Cure,** and **45 Grave.** I was also delving into much heavier bands, like **Slayer, Formicide, Exodus, Celtic Frost.** This pattern of style-whoring continued through the '90s. Some standouts from that period, would be **Tad, Aphex Twin,** Tricky, Marilyn Manson, **Far, Deftones, Handsome Family,** and **Deadsy.** Yet, like some giant monstrosity from a B-movie, I found that I retained pieces and facts about all of these musicians and bands I listened to, their work almost becoming a part of my very personality.

Now, here I am approaching 40, and I still love music and horror. The list of artists that walk the line between those two things I love so dearly is long...and stylistically all over the place. But it isn't all about killers and monsters and creepy crawlies...some of those bands just write some seriously dark shit. **Thought Industry, Paper Chase, Swans, Godflesh**—c'mon! What say you, Simon?

# IN THE TEETH OF THE WOLF

Where the hell do I even begin? I'm going to have to take a slight detour, so bear with me please.

According to my mom, I was a slightly odd child, apparently visiting the local cemetery on a regular basis at age three with my Dad and then building, at age six, miniature headstones and grave-markers out of kids' plastic building-blocks and laying them out in the garden. Given that, I was into really dark, terrifying music from an early age, right? Well, no.

My first encounter with "morbid music," all the way back in 1973, was the British re-release of **Bobby "Boris" Pickett and the Crypt-Kickers'** 1962 novelty song "Monster Mash." It was indeed a Graveyard Smash with this ten-year-old boy. I got into so-called *krautrock* around the same time or, more specifically, the Berlin School of Rock, listening to artists like **Tangerine Dream,** Klaus Schulze and others of that ilk. Despite their *kosmische musik* stylings and noodlings, I always felt there was something darker waiting in the wings, something I would now describe as Lovecraftian, just waiting for when the stars came right and they would emerge in all their multi-tentacled, squamous and eldritchly hideous glory.

I had to wait another two decades before I discovered the bastard offspring of those early '70s electronic instrumental groups, in the form of the first wave of industrial projects, like **Throbbing Gristle, Nurse with Wound, Current 93, Coil,** and the dark folkways of **Sol Invictus.** That was *after* the phase where I got into the obligatory heavy-metal scene (**Judas Priest,** anyone?), then thrash and speed metal—by way of bands like **Agnostic Front, English Dogs** and Billy Milano's **S.O.D.**—and finally landing on the shores of the lands inhabited by **Slayer** (south of Heaven, apparently), **Megadeth, Metallica, Venom,** and tons of obscure, one-album-wonder bands whose names I have, mercifully, forgotten.

After a time I wandered into the quieter cathedrals of the goth scene, throwing arms and confetti waiflike into the air to **The Cult, The Mission,** and **The Fields of the Nephilim,** before breaking out and streaking into bloody **Skinny Puppy, Frontline Assembly,** and **KMFDM** territory. Only to circle back and find myself in a place where my industrial roots were showing once again—except now we're talking **Kerovnian, TenHornedBeast, Nordvargr, MZ412, Archon Satani,** and the magnificent **Deadwood,** in addition to the ones who had gone before. And how I loved **Godflesh** and **Ministry.** I even went and formed my own record label, FracturedSpacesRecords, in the wake of my renewed interest in dark ambient and noise rock, but that's a story for another time...

## A MIND OF FLESH AND BONES

So, there you have it—a brief résumé of our collective musical credentials. No doubt about it, we are both stuck steadfast in the darkness of the sonic abyss, residing at markedly different depths yet sharing the same sense that somehow these particular genres speak to our souls and resonate with our experiences of the wider world and life itself.

So come and join us on our walk along that rocky road, as we shed light into the shadowed corners and dig up the coal-encrusted gems that are scattered throughout the darker seams of music. Explore with us the idea that herein lie, perhaps, greater truths than in any of the lightweight pap that gets thrust upon us by the media barons of MTV, the "music press" and the hundreds of other media outlets now extant. It's either that, or it could just be that we're a pair of old grumpy, morbid buggers...

Yeah, it's probably that.

**John Boden** resides in the shadow of Three Mile Island with his wonderful wife and children. Aside from his work with *Shock Totem,* his stories can be found or are forthcoming in *52 Stitches, Everyday Weirdness,* and *Black Ink Horror #7.*

**Simon Marshall-Jones** is a UK-based writer, artist, editor, publisher and blogger: also wine and cheese lover, music freak and covered in too many tattoos.

# Stitched

by Christopher Green

Jacob's Mother would have told him not to pick at it. But he'd done as he'd been told too often, and now she, too, was gone.

She'd taken him to the doctor once a week, and once she'd vanished he continued to go. It was what she would have wanted.

He sat in the doctors' waiting room, next to a coffee table scattered with old magazines.

The receptionist smiled at him when he met her eyes, and he looked away, at each of the three doors to her left. The doctors had introduced themselves to him at the start of every visit for sixteen years, but Jacob still liked his own names for them better.

Doctor Poke's door was in the middle. He always had something in his hands, something cold and metallic and designed to pull something out of you or push something into you. His office smelled like dead air, and everything in it was slick. When Jacob was younger, he'd needed help to climb onto the table, and even when he got there he knew if he leaned forward too much, if he kicked or squirmed, he'd slip right off the table and onto the floor, and no one would bother to catch him.

He and Doctor Poke did not get along, and Doctor Poke had run Jacob through his gauntlet and passed him on to Doctor Listen.

Doctor Listen's door was farthest from the receptionist, tucked back in the corner near the cramped toilet where Doctor Poke used to send him for samples.

He'd spent years with Doctor Listen, and he liked him the best, by far. The lights weren't often on, and the windows were usually open a crack, which let tram noise and the buzz of the street below drift wherever it liked. The room was warm, Doctor Listen's desk was full of interesting gadgets that quietly whirred or ticked or spun, and Doctor Listen didn't try to do anything beyond understand him.

After many lengthy one-sided conversations, Doctor Listen had referred him to Doctor Tell, whom he waited for now.

Jacob's watch beeped at him to tell him it was one o'clock and time for his appointment, and the receptionist glanced up and shrugged. Dr. Tell would be late again. Jacob resisted the urge to slide the razor from its place in the pocket of his polo shirt and stood up instead. He folded his hands in front of him, like a preacher just before the big silver plate gets passed around, and walked over to her.

"Excuse me," he said. She'd already stopped writing, but she waited a beat longer than he would have liked to set down her pen and tilt her face up at him.

"Yes, Mr. Mevra?"

"Do you know how much longer Dr. Tell will be with his other patient?"

She blinked, and he could see her put an answer together from the pile of words she was allowed to use with him. "Dr. Gillespie will be with you as soon as he can, Mr. Mevra. It shouldn't be too much longer."

"My appointment is for one o'clock," Jacob said, tapping his watch gently with a manicured fingernail and nodding at the clock behind her. "I can only wait an hour, and then I'll have to reschedule." He knew as soon as the words left his mouth that he shouldn't have said anything.

The receptionist nodded. "Of course, Mr. Mevra. Would you like to take a seat?"

It was Jacob's turn to nod, and for a moment their heads bobbed at each other like birds in the middle of some ritual. He turned back toward the leather chairs and the coffee table and the magazines, then paused and faced her once again. "I wonder, miss, if I might be able to borrow a piece of paper?"

She smiled and tore one from the pad she'd been writing on, one page below the one she'd been using. He thanked her and returned to his seat.

He passed the next twenty minutes by simply running the pads of his fingers along the edge of the paper, but it wasn't enough. The room was getting darker. Every once in a while he would look over at the receptionist and she wouldn't be there.

Jacob could make out words on the paper, words that had pressed through to it from the paper above. Words the receptionist had been writing, ones not in the pile she was allowed to use with him in casual conversation. Like crazy, or cutter, or compulsive. "C" words. His father would have had another "C" word for her, and probably the "A" one and the "F" one and the "MF" one, too, but his father had vanished long ago. He was one of the few Jacob didn't feel guilty about.

When Jacob started letting the paper bite a bit deeper, the receptionist was gone less often. She was biting her lip and eyeing the blood on the edge of Jacob's borrowed piece of paper. Jacob didn't care what she thought. If he stopped she'd be gone for good, like his mother, like his father, like countless others. The receptionist was nice to look at and smelled like vanilla and, when he was younger, had taken his temperature or his blood with her soft, cool hands.

He dragged the edge of the paper along the cuts in his fingers. When the paper became too soaked in blood he turned it to another edge. By a quarter to two, he'd had to resort to neatly tearing his own edges into the paper, holding it against the edge of the coffee table and being as quiet as he could during the ripping part. The receptionist watched him openly, now, but he was careful, and wiped his fingers with his handkerchief, and used the hand that wasn't cut to pick things up or set them down. She was always there, now, whenever he looked up, and that was enough.

Dr. Tell finally opened his office door at two o'clock, and Jacob knew he'd been correct. Let Dr. Tell know you were willing to wait an hour, and you were certain to be waiting an hour.

The receptionist opened her mouth, but Jacob was already on his feet. He brushed past Dr. Tell and went to his usual spot inside the office, in the wooden chair with the wooden rungs with the wooden knobs that stuck into his back when he shifted position, across from the Doctor's long, empty desk.

Dr. Tell closed the door and sat on his side of the desk.

The little slashes on Jacob's fingertips had stopped bleeding. He steepled his fingers and watched the doctor. The old scars along his hands were pale in the tiny office lights that shone down on them like stars.

"Thank you for you patience, Jacob. I had some other business to attend to."

"What kind of business?"

Dr. Tell's Adam's apple bobbed in and out of his collar when he swallowed, like a buoy in rough seas. "Pardon me?"

"What kind of business is so important that you leave me sitting out there for an hour? You say I'm a sick man, Dr. Tell, but you don't treat me like I'm sick. You treat me like I'm stupid."

"I don't think you're stupid, Jacob, I think you need help."

Jacob nodded. "I believe that. But you say I need the kind of help that only you can give me. Dr. Poke thought that for a few years. Dr. Listen thought that for a decade. How long before you change your mind, too?"

Dr. Tell sighed. "I won't change my mind, Jacob."

"Because the only explanation left will be mine? One day, then, that'll be the only thing left. You can tell and tell and tell, or poke and poke, or listen and listen, and you won't change the truth of it."

Dr. Tell sat back in his chair and ran his thumbs over his eyebrows, for a moment, and then tried again. "Let us use logic, then, shall we? Yes? To dissect the problem before us."

"All right."

"You, Jacob Mevra, are convinced the world will end if you don't cut yourself and stitch yourself back up. Correct?"

"Well, it won't end, I guess. The world will keep right on spinning, if that's what you mean, but there won't be anyone left to enjoy it."

Dr. Tell nodded emphatically. "Understood. Yet, here we are, and you aren't cutting yourself right this moment, are you?"

"No," Jacob said, "because I did it in the waiting room. I had to, before your receptionist slid away. We should be okay for a little while, but it wasn't much, so it won't last for very long."

"But you've gone for long periods without cutting yourself, haven't you? I know you have. I know Dr. "Poke" prescribed sedatives and your mother assured us that you didn't so much as get out of bed for two weeks."

Jacob shifted in his chair and, sure enough, the wooden knobs ground against his spine. "I did what I could, then. I remember biting my tongue, or the insides of my mouth. But it wasn't enough. That was when the boy across the street slid away, and the man who used to run the dry cleaner, and the woman who used to bag our groceries."

"But these people, can you be sure they existed?"

Jacob shifted position again. He hated this part of his conversations with Dr.

Tell. "I can be sure, I guess, but I don't know how to make you sure of it. Or of me. Someone else bagged our groceries, a different guy took my Mom's dresses at the dry cleaner, and the house across the street never had a little boy, after that, and the parents didn't miss him."

"You mean they didn't care, that they looked for him for a little while and then stopped?"

Jacob's fingertip itched, and he knew that soon he'd have to start again. "No. I mean that the boy just never was, and his parents didn't know it. They didn't know of him, and so they couldn't miss him."

Dr. Tell smiled so widely that Jacob could see the teeth at the sides of his mouth. "Exactly. Do you know what the word *manifestation* means, Jacob. As in, this cutting, of yours, is a physical *manifestation* of an otherwise mental disorder?"

"It means you think it's a clue, that I cut my skin and stitch it back together and that means that, inside, where you can't poke or listen or tell, something else is wrong with me."

"Correct. That's exactly right." Dr. Tell looked very pleased with himself.

Jacob shook his head and smiled his own little smile. "Well, how about this? I think you are incapable of belief. Not once, in the years and years of consultations, have any of you even once considered that maybe I'm not crazy. Maybe I'm right. I think that's a *manifestation* of your own pigheadedness. When you're a hammer, all the world's a nail, am I right?" Jacob stood.

Dr. Tell did, too. "Jacob, don't go, yet."

"I have to. I have things to do."

"Cuts to make? Wounds to stitch?"

"Yes."

"Please, Jacob, don't."

"Answer me this, Doctor. If I see *you* fading next time, if it isn't some little boy or some old lady or your receptionist, *then* do you want me to stop? Is *that* when I should decide that I'm wrong and you're right and tuck my hands quietly into my pockets and watch you vanish and come into a waiting room where there are two doors instead of three, or maybe three doors and this one's used by someone else, a Doctor who swears he's been seeing me for years and that there never was a Dr. Tell. Is *that* when you want me to stop? Or is that the one time when I should make a few little cuts, just to be certain?"

Dr. Tell flinched, and opened his mouth a few times, and said nothing.

Jacob got to the door and yanked it open. There was a mother and her child in the waiting room, anxiously checking her watch and looking at Dr. Poke's door.

"You know what, Doctor," Jacob said, and stepped back into the office, closing the door behind him. It wasn't anything a child needed to know. "You asked me, way back when, if I did all this because God asked me to."

"I remember that, yes. You said he didn't"

"God didn't come in to it at all. The Devil, he's the one. Sat next to me, one day, a little after I'd worked it out, after I knew how to make things not slide away, sat right down next to me, that Devil, and asked me *not* to. I couldn't tell my mother that she'd picked the Devil's side."

Jacob left.

The pads of Dr. Tell's fingertips itched so badly he wanted to scratch at them until they bled.

**Christopher Green** was born in the United States and moved to Australia at the age of 20, after meeting his wife on the Internet (she wasn't his wife at the time). He attended Clarion South in 2007 and therein found the crucible he needed, like-minded authors who didn't flinch at talk of autopsies, alien implants, and the evolutionary purpose of elf ears. His fiction has been published in *Dreaming Again, Beneath Ceaseless Skies,* and *Abyss & Apex.* He lives in Geelong with his wife and their two perpetually muddy Labradors.

Visit him on his blog at **christophergreen.wordpress.com**.

# RUTH ACROSS THE SEA

### by Steven Pirie

Ruth coughs: this close, she thinks she can *taste* the Executioner's breath. He's a small man down here in his dark lair, unmasked and away from the height and fear of the gallows' stage. He stinks of stale urine and semen. There's the hint of an erection under his stained gown.

"This is the rope?" says Ruth. It's heavy, and the noose is more rigid than she imagined. She wonders how so stiff a knot can be tightened to fit a victim's neck. Surely a rope this tight would jerk the head clean off.

The Executioner grins. His teeth are blackened and broken. "Best ropes as can be found, lady," he says. "As sure as sure to snap the bones first time."

"Is that your aim, to kill by breaking the neck?"

"No, lady." The Executioner breathes heavily. He fumbles briefly under his gowns. His face is flushed. "Not if I can help it. I like them to die on the drawing. I like their eyes bulging when I show them their innards."

Ruth looks away. A fire burns in a great hearth. The flames cast a Hellish hue to the Executioner's den. Its dull light flickers upon the ornate handle of a razor.

"They tell me your victims dance before dying, that they fling themselves upon the noose to be sure to break the neck. A cleaner, quicker death than drawing, I'm told."

"Ah, but these are *my* ropes," says the Executioner. "No one knows these ropes like me, and only I can say who dances and who breaks on the end of them."

Ruth reaches for the razor. Its blade is blue sharp; its handle encrusted with diamonds and gems. She marvels at how balanced it is in her grasp. Ruth draws breath.

"I want you to slice part way through the rope. When we dance tomorrow, I want the rope to snap, do you understand?"

The Executioner grins once more. "It can be arranged, Lady, for a certain payment."

"Oh?"

The Executioner pulls open his gowns. Ruth thinks she might swoon with the stench. She reaches down and grips the Executioner's penis. He grunts and grins up at her.

"Arrange it," says Ruth. With her other hand, she presses the razor against the Executioner's scrotum. His grin wavers for an instant, but he loses none of his erection. "Arrange it, or the price will be all yours."

"That's tough talk, lady." The Executioner reaches down also, so both now hold the razor against his skin. He draws Ruth's hand slowly to the side, and Ruth feels blood on her palm. "Maybe I like it tough. But you have a plan, no? You have thoughts of rescue and escape, perhaps?"

Ruth shivers. The Executioner places both palms upon Ruth's shoulders and presses her downward to her knees. His penis stares out at her with its one good eye. She knows what he wants, though she's never done such a thing.

"There are those who are hanged themselves for such thoughts," he says. He draws Ruth's head forwards. "But be nice to me, lady, and perhaps tomorrow's dance really will be brief."

~

Later, as the sun sets beyond the castle ramparts, Ruth stands alone upon the west turret. Beyond the paddock and the woods, the sun is golden on the sea. The masts of a galleon are black against the sky. In her mind, Ruth hears the creaking of its timbers. Gulls wheel as the bow wave tumbles. With the snapping of the sails, she tastes the salt spray of the open sea.

She licks her lips, but it's a different salt that lingers. In the courtyard, Ruth sees the Executioner upon his scaffold. He has buckets for the guts, and guttering for the blood. As he attaches the ropes he glances up at her and grins.

Ruth sighs. What price is freedom in the promise of a dawn so terrible?

~

The drumbeats begin before the sun rises. They start slowly, steady like the day's heartbeat. An early mist has fallen, and it seems to Ruth the world beyond the town gates no longer exists.

At the gallows, Ruth stands to the side, away from the bustle of the crowd. The cart, stacked with blankets, cost her five guineas. The horse cost her all the money she'd saved. The sailors who would fight for the diversion, and then see her safely across the sea, cost Ruth her virginity. Ruth shudders remembering how she'd lain back and closed her eyes as one by one they'd *loved* her. They were not gentle lovers—they had a sea farer's urgency—and she was dry and virgin-tight. And then there came the pain of gin and scalding baths to kill the seeds inside her. She'd say *cleansing* baths, though she doubts she'll feel clean again.

A herald sounds, and the prisoners are led to the gallows. They're gaunt and beaten, too spent to do anything but trudge to their fate. The drums are silent as the ropes are placed about their necks. The crowd is still. The Executioner's hood billows with his rapid breathing. He pulls the lever and the crowd roars. The sailors shove and push. A shout is heard. A punch is thrown. The prisoners dance on their ropes. But not for long; the executioner has his razor to wield. There are *live* guts to be spilled.

And in the roar and confusion, a rope snaps. A prisoner *thuds* to the ground and is rolled to the side. The cart is waiting, the blankets pulled back. Ruth climbs in also. A whip raps against horse flesh. The cart rocks forward toward the sea.

"You see," says Ruth, "I said I'll be here for you."

Ruth nuzzles in to her lover; feels the softness of her breast against her face.

Mary can barely speak.

"Hush. Today we go across the sea," says Ruth, "To where a woman can love a woman without fear of death."

**Steven Pirie** lives in Liverpool, England with his wife Ann and their son James.

His fiction has appeared in many magazines and anthologies around the world. His comic fantasy novel, *Digging up Donald,* published by **Immanion Press,** has attracted excellent reviews. A new novel, **Burying Brian,** will be published by **Immanion Press** in December, 2010.

Details of all this and more may be found at **www.stevenpirie.com.**

# Duval Street

by Mekenzie Larsen

I walk down Whitehead Street with eight bucks and a cigarette lighter in the right pocket of my overcoat and a travel-size can of hairspray in the left. Not out of fear or necessity. Old habit is all, and what habit could be harder to break than the desire to protect oneself? Drugs, I suppose, or sex; but I'm not fit to make a proper comparison as I've had neither. So I continue to carry my means of defense. You can never be too careful, as my Nana used to say, with so many creeps in the world.

I squint against the light that finds its way through the cracks in my veil. Aside from the God-awful sun, it's a charming day. The squawking of parrots and the squealing of the children feeding them against all posted requests drifts to my ears on wind that smells of booze and sweat masked by cheap floral perfume. Lilac or violet? I can never tell the difference. It smells purple, either way. I stroll past tourist shops and million-dollar houses. The Audubon gardens look especially green today, the leaves and stems of yellow blossoms almost too crisp for my eyes to take in under this bastard sun. The house coming up on my right appears empty, though the yard is cropped and the porch recently waxed. Sandra Bullock's, you know. The trolley guide told us as much. I pass Hemingway's old home, which, I've been told, is overrun with six-toed cats named after fallen movie stars. I like to tell people I have six toes. "Really?" they will ask. "On which foot?" No, no, no, I say. I have six toes *altogether*. They stare back at me until I begin to laugh and soon they're laughing, too, but I know they're curling their toes uncomfortably inside their expensive, polished shoes.

I stand at the corner of Whitehead and Truman, my head down and my hands in my pockets. A dark-skinned woman in a hot pink mesh top and cutoff denim shorts steps up beside me, humming along to Jimmy Buffet whose voice drones on and on from all directions. Which song she's attempting to keep the beat to, I can't tell. I fidget with the lighter inside my coat and contemplate setting myself on fire right there on the corner, another attraction, another freak. I would blend right in with the other flamers. Ha! I let the lighter drop further into my pocket and curl my hand into a ball which takes some effort due to the garish length of my nails. Smile, for chrissakes, and don't make it look so forced. Show some teeth.

The dark-skinned woman takes one look at me and makes a mad dash for an open door across the street. She nearly gets clipped by a speeding scooter and I shout after her, "Better luck next time, sweetie!" I doubt she could see my face through all this crackled rayon but the possibility still makes me tingle. I'm grinning like a clown who's tangled with a Chelsea gang.

Too many creeps in the world, by God; one too many to count.

The sidewalk disappears under my skirt a foot at a time, swallowed then spit from the heels of my boots. A pirate brushes past me in a cloud of smoke too sweet and too pungent to be anything but hash. "'Scuse me, ma'am." I don't have anything to gain by correcting him so I glare after him instead, knowing he feels me watching him, hoping he looks back. He doesn't.

I round the curb. A trolley rolls by, bells ringing. I count five passengers, each of them snapping pictures with cheap plastic cameras that only a tourist would carry. The last cruise ship party, I bet, making another round for souvenirs they passed over or coming ashore after spending the day on their cabin balcony, tipsy on sea air, with no intention of leaving the ship but twenty minutes before it leaves port deciding what the hell, let's risk it, they can't all be wasted or queer.

People have no sense of adventure.

Duval Street is bustling as usual. I pause to admire my reflection in a window and smirk at the expression on the shopkeeper's face. Whether it's my presence or not, something sends him round the counter and out of sight. What's the matter, doll? Never seen a widower before? I sigh and move on, snatching an orange from a produce cart. It joins the lighter in my coat pocket. The cart caddy doesn't so much as look up from the paper he's so keen on finishing. The light here is angrier, if you can believe it, harsher. I can feel it tearing through the layers of black rayon and supple leather to gnaw at my war-torn skin. My body is a battleground, an old one, yet I don't wear protection. Never have. I think it's cruel to tell people that slathering themselves with SPF-whatever will protect them from the sky's burning asshole. Look at my Nana. Wore sunscreen every day of her life. Wore long sleeves most of the year. She even started carrying one of those cute, frilly parasols (got some stares for that one, she did, but we were quite used to them by then). Dead at 28. Skin cancer. Genetics, they had said. So what good does the suckscreen do, besides leaving you smelling like a plastic houseplant?

Still pale as milk when she went, though. I guess I can give it that.

Everything around me is a blur, a spin cycle of brilliant colors—red, sky blue, sea blue, lime, vermillion, yellow—against stark white (the suckscreen at work), orange, and brown skin. Here is the gaggle of parrots I heard before, some pruning, some strutting about the sidewalk. No sign of the children with their hands full of chip crumbs and pieces of soggy burger buns. Across the street stands a hunchbacked man in more stereotypical pirate regalia, posing for snapshots. I can't tell whether the hump is fake or not. I have no doubt his teeth are. Walking two steps in front of me is a young blonde, baked, her halter revealing black angel-wings faded blue stamped across her shoulder blades, a cell phone pressed to her ear. "No, I don't like the lobster. Can't we get the buffet, instead? No, I'm on Duval. Where is that again? A left? Wait a minute, something's going on ..."

The girl's pace slows and I slow behind her. A crowd has formed about five yards ahead, just past a sign that proclaims "Fresh Fish! Live Music! Open Late!" in smudged pink chalk. *Must be some good fish,* I think, and I almost plow into the blonde who has come to a complete stop. "Sheena," she's saying, "I'll have to call you back."

I move around the blonde, now nervously twisting her ponytail through her fingers, and join the crowd which is quickly becoming a mob of sweaty hands on shoulders and bony elbows in ribs. Even in six inch heels, I can't see what the fuss is all about. I straighten my veil and prepare to turn away when a woman steps out onto the balcony directly above us, looks down, and screams. Their collective daze broken, most of them step back to crane their heads in the woman's direction. I take the opportunity to squeeze my way through to stand at the center of their circle. I'm just as confused as I had been seconds before.

A deer lays crumpled on its side, its head turned away, its neck broken. Its hind legs have been replaced with those of a man. Its front legs are human arms. Caucasian. Toned. Undoubtedly from the same body. But whose? I'm more fascinated by the wind-up device protruding from the poor beast's back, huge, gold-plated. Definitely handmade. I have never seen a mechanism that size, like something that should be attached to Big Ben. I lift my skirt and step over the body to examine it from the other side, careful not to trip over what appears to be the remnants of a gator tail sewn haphazardly to the buck's rear. A stained shot glass stares back at me. The other socket is hidden behind a felt eyepatch. My fingers itch to peel it away, but I resist and dig my nails further into my palm. I run the toe of my boot over the stitches that run the length of its belly. Gutted, too. Just another person's fucked up idea of a science project.

The mob is growing larger and more vocal.

"Jesus, where did it come from?"

"Somebody call the cops!"

"Mommy? *It smells.*"

A gentleman in a suit vomits into his hands, spraying his shoes and the bare feet of the woman beside him. She shrieks in disgust and bats him with her purse. "Sick!" As if walking the streets of Old Town sans shoes is the epitome of good hygiene.

"Did anyone see anything?" A man is scribbling something down in a notepad. His glasses, which are far too large for his face, have slid dangerously close to the tip of his nose and he pushes them back with one finger. "How do you imagine it got here?"

"Don't know, man."

"Well, it certainly didn't walk..."

"Where's the rest of the body?"

*Which one?*

Too many people. Too many questions. Too much interest in this mad scientist's experiment gone awry. I feel bad for the chap. Days, maybe weeks spent measuring and sawing and stitching, draining and ditching. I can't imagine investing that kind of time and energy and expecting no credit in return. They will probably mount the fucker and display it in a museum, a preserved piece of creativity conceivable only by that small demographic of mortals that includes cannibals, serial killers, and momma's boys. The hand-crafted wind-up says it all. Real love went into this thing, this caricature of how Dali may have pictured

Santa's reindeer. I wonder if he's watching us. I wonder if his art will ever get the recognition it deserves.

An ambulance pulls up in silence, one wheel parked on the sidewalk. The driver shouts from the window for everyone to go home. Nobody moves. It will be another hour before the mob begins to thin. Young men in starched white uniforms are bringing round a stretcher.

This is where I draw the line.

I retreat the way I came, past the parrots and the neon signs, past the waxed porch where Sandra Bullock may or may not have stood that morning, coffee in hand. I walk past all the bleached teeth, fried hair, and through the side door of the bed-and-breakfast where I'm booked until Friday. The air conditioning is a welcome change. I remove my veil, my wig, my boots. I toss everything onto the bed and pour myself a drink.

There's always Miami Beach.

**Mekenzie Larsen** lives in a hole that she dug herself in the northern Mississippi backwoods. She has the dirt under her nails to prove it. Her free time is spent concocting potions, detangling her hair, and teaching feral cats to walk a tight rope.

# Mr. Many Faces

by S. Clayton Rhodes

-1-

If there was one thing Eric Forshey knew, it was that there weren't any bug-eyed bugaboos in Audra's room. Not lurking behind the curtains or squeezed beneath her bed.

Rubbing the predawn sand from his eyes, he opened the walk-in closet door. "Nothing. See?" Audra's school jumpers, sweaters, and jeans dangled from hangers. On the shelves overhead, stuffed animals—pandas, ducks and sock monkeys—looked down with fixed, glassy expressions. But there were no slavering ghouls with steely fangs.

Audra had her comforter pulled taut to her chin. "But he was there, Daddy," she insisted. "He *was.*"

Eric nodded. "Okay. Suppose you tell me what this thing looked like."

Audra shivered. "He was dark and wrinkled...and wore necklaces of human teeth. You wouldn't believe how many teeth were on those necklaces! And his eyes were all runny. Like when you don't cook our eggs all the way."

Eric didn't care for the critique on his cooking but knew what she meant. "Anything else?"

Audra let her covers drop a bit. "Uh-huh. He smelled like dead fish, made squishy sounds when he moved, and...oh, yeah, he had *lots* of faces."

Eric furrowed his brow at this new twist. "Lots of faces? You mean all over his body?"

"No, he kept the extras in this bag around his shoulder. Like a purse."

"All right, I think we're getting somewhere. Did this guy show you these extra faces? Did he tell you about them?"

"No, I started yelling for you the second he opened the door."

Eric rose and flicked off the overhead light, which caused instant shrieks from Audra.

"Turn it back on, Daddy! Turn it back on!"

He flipped the switch again. "Don't worry, kiddo. I'm still here. Just wanted to prove something."

Audra looked doubtful.

Eric sent the room back into blackness once more. "Now," he said, "how many fingers am I holding up?"

"Daddy, it's so dark in here I can't tell."

"Exactly, Audra. It's too dark to say." The light came back on. "You must have been waking up from a bad dream, honey. How else could you see something in the dark, even if it *had* been here? And how could you know what this thing had in his bag?"

"I just *knew*," she said with quiet insistence.

"Sure. You just knew because that's the way it is in dreams."

Because she didn't appear entirely convinced, Eric got one of the animals down from the closet shelf—a dopey stuffed rabbit with matted ears. Now that Audra was eight, it rarely saw the light of day.

"Why don't you sleep with this guy tonight? Might make you feel better."

Audra accepted the rabbit and clutched it close. "Can I leave a light on?"

"Oh, Audra, I don't think you'd get much sleep—"

"Please, Daddy. I'll sleep. Just don't make me sleep in the dark."

"Okay, hang on a sec." He went out to the hall closet, rummaging until finding a lower wattage bulb to use in her Barbie lamp.

"How's that?"

Audra grinned. "Perfect!"

-2-

Downstairs, Eric poured a few fingers of sloe gin into something resembling a clean glass. He knocked it back with purpose then poured another for good measure.

Jesus, why did Audra have to scream that way? It was hard enough getting to sleep now that he and Meredith had split. A year later and he still couldn't get used to a half-empty bed.

He supposed he'd deserved everything he got, though. He hadn't been much of a husband, so it wasn't surprising when Meredith asked him for a divorce. Ultimately, their life had been anything but perfect, and parting ways seemed the only answer.

Then the fight for Audra had begun. Funny, but Eric hadn't realized how much the little rugrat meant to him until he faced losing her.

After nine tense months, he'd wound up with joint custody. Meredith kept the house, while Eric had taken up residence in a duplex near the railroad tracks on the west side—all he could afford, given lawyer fees and child support while waiting on the final decision. He ended up staying on there. It could use a woman's touch, but then he wasn't likely to meet anyone new, employed as he was as a shift worker across the river.

Speaking of which, he really should be getting some sleep instead of staying up, trying to make some sort of sense of the world through the bottom of a gin glass.

He set the glass in the sink, a new friend for the unwashed dishes, then trudged back upstairs.

-3-

Eric made it back to town at a quarter past five, but instead of going straight home, he stopped in at the Langtree Tavern. He couldn't believe it, but he'd muffed yet another job today, and a cold mug or two would do wonders in taking away the edge. As for Audra, Mrs. Mayhew from next door would feed her some supper if he didn't show soon. Audra was practically the granddaughter Mrs. Mayhew had never known, and they both looked for excuses to spend time together anyhow.

So he knocked back a few and shot some pool. When he looked at the neon clock on the wall above the bar, he was surprised to see it was 7:05. How the hell had it gotten so late?

-4-

There weren't any lights on downstairs, so he supposed Audra was still next door. He was about to knock on the Mayhews' door when he heard water running upstairs. Audra must be getting ready for bed. Probably brushing her teeth before her final TV session and twenty minutes of reading.

The kitchen counter was littered with breadcrumbs, and smears of peanut butter from where Audra had made her supper. Apparently she hadn't eaten next door.

Eventually, Audra came down, wearing a unicorn nightie and smelling of strawberry shampoo.

"Hi, Daddy." She took one of his hands in hers and leaned into the armrest of the recliner.

Eric muted the sitcom rerun he'd been looking at but not really watching. "Hey, sweetheart. D'you do your homework?"

She nodded. "A little math and some spelling words we had to put into sentences. How was work?"

He laughed. "How is it ever? Rotten."

"Do you want me to fix you something to eat, Daddy? I'm learning to cook."

He smiled at the offer, thinking of the peanut butter sandwich she'd made earlier. "No thanks, baby. Daddy had a sandwich already." The last two hours were admittedly a bit of a blur, but he had vague memories of eating something at the Langtree.

"Okay," she said, and curled up on the edge of the couch, watching him going back to not really watching the show.

-5-

When 3:15 arrived, it came with the same screams from Audra as the night before. When Eric reached her doorway and flicked on the light, her breath came in ragged hitches as she pointed at the closet door. The door was closed, but this time a tiny purse hanging by its strap on the doorknob rocked from side to side.

"Mr. Many Faces!" she gasped. "Mr. Many Faces was here again, Daddy. And he said he was going to take me to a dark place where I'd never ever see you again!"

He considered calling Meredith to ask her if Audra had shown any similar problems at her house, but if he did, Meredith would press for details. Audra had to be doing this for attention and Meredith would demand to know why. Was he spending too much time playing pool with his buddies again? Ignoring his fatherly duties?

And of course now the creature from her closet had a name. Mr. Many Faces.

He had, according to Audra, invited her to try on one of his rubbery spare faces, having made it halfway to her bed this time just before threatening to take her away.

Instead of calling Meredith, after work the next night Eric stopped by a hardware store and picked up a hook-and-eye latch. He'd spend some extra one-on-one time with Audra, thinking if he did that she wouldn't feel neglected, wouldn't feel the need for attention in the middle of the night.

Audra wasn't home when he got there, but she'd see his car and would be over any time. Eric cranked on the oven and brushed ice from a Banquet chicken dinner and, sure enough, Audra showed up as he was shoving supper onto the rack.

"You already eat?" he asked.

She nodded. "Mrs. Mayhew had beef stroganoff and rolls."

"Sounds delish." A sight better than what he was having, for sure.

While they were waiting on his meal, they went up to Audra's room, where she watched in rapt attention as Eric installed the latch on the closet door.

"This," Eric said, "will keep Mr. Many Faces right where he belongs."

He made a point of asking how school was, and after he ate they played two hands of Old Maid. Then, instead of letting her read on her own for the last twenty minutes, Eric scooted onto the bed beside her and read to her while smoothing her wheat-colored hair.

Back downstairs, he cracked a Coors and thumbed through the mail—mostly bills. He must have been more tired than he imagined, because he drifted off in the recliner, ESPN buzzing in the background.

Awakened some hours later by Audra's screams, he bounded up the stairs and threw open the door. Audra was out of bed and hugging his waist before he was all the way in the room.

He saw what the problem was. She had pried the hook and eye latch off the closet door. Hard to believe she had that kind of strength, but of course that was what had happened. She'd gone that extra step in trying to prove Mr. Many Faces was a living, breathing thing. This time, what looked to be damp footprints trailed across the carpet.

Eric glanced around for whatever she'd used to lever off the latch. He didn't spot a screwdriver or any sponge she might've used to create the watery tracks. What *did* attract his attention, though, was Audra's stuffed bunny, Flopsy. Or, more accurately, the *pieces* of it. Its bucktoothed head rested against a Barbie Dream House, while the body leaked cotton batting from its stump of a neck.

There was an odd smell, too. Something like decaying fish and the kind of dark silt you'd find at the bottom of a stagnant pond, dim and gassy.

He wondered briefly if Audra hadn't opened a can of tuna and left it to rot to further validate her story. Monsters always stank.

Audra didn't try to convince him that Mr. Many Faces was real this go-round. She merely said, "Please, Daddy. *Please* can I sleep in your room tonight?"

He knew it wasn't a good idea, a grown man letting his eight-year-old sleep with him. Meredith would have a field day if she found out, raising all the allegations she could. And on top of that, he was no psychologist but knew it might do more harm than good to give in.

In spite of everything, he heard himself say, "Okay, pumpkin, let's go to Daddy's room."

-7-

Visitation exchanges occurred on Saturdays, whenever possible. The routine was to take Audra to the Lincoln County Library and leave her in the children's section under the watch of one of the matronly librarians working that area who knew them. There was no danger in leaving her under their supervision. The arrangement was good since he and Meredith didn't even have to cross paths.

"She's just going to play some games on one of the computers," he told Mrs. Raylin.

"That's just fine, Mr. Forshey," she said with something like a pitying smile. "We'll look after her."

Eric always got a little choked up. No matter how many times they went through this, it never stopped feeling as though it might be the last time he'd see Audra.

"Be good," he told her.

"I will."

"And mind your mother."

"Sure."

"And—"

"And eat everything on my plate. Even the green things. I know."

"Sure, you do," he said, kissing her wisp of bangs. "Love you, pumpkin."

"I love you, too, Daddy."

-8-

Open confessionals at St. Michael's started at 3:00. Eric hadn't been to confession in ages but felt he ought to now. There had to be something he was doing wrong with Audra, something he was missing. Maybe talking it over with someone would help him sort it out.

He pulled to the curb and headed for the slab of stairs. Inside, the church was empty and dark. No candles were lit.

Crossing himself, Eric thought, *Spectacles, testicles, wallet and watch.* Never had it seemed so irreverent as now, and his footfalls were incredibly loud from vestibule to vaulted ceiling.

He entered one side of the confessional and crossed himself again while staring at the wicker grating. It took only a moment before the tiny wooden partition slid open. Next came the shallow, nasally breathing of the priest.

"I am ready," the priest said. It was Father Hogan, if Eric wasn't mistaken.

"Forgive me, Father, for I have sinned."

"How long has it been since your last confession, my son?"

"I'm not sure, Father. A year ago?"

"Please go on." Another nasally breath of air.

Eric wanted to move forward with his admission, but he wasn't sure what sin he'd even committed, if any. Thinking maybe it would be better just to let the priest figure it out, he heard himself blurt, "Is it a sin, Father, to be passive toward your child?"

"I'm not sure I take your meaning, my son."

"Sorry, Father. I love my daughter, but sometimes I think maybe I don't spend enough time with her."

Nasally air in. Whistling air out. "I wouldn't say that it is a sin. Of course if it gets to the point of neglect, you would be in the wrong. Unformed minds need an adult presence for direction. But that is a matter of parenting. If you'd like to make a counseling appointment—"

"No, no, Father. I'd prefer to be heard out now, if you're agreeable."

Though he couldn't see the priest, Eric imagined he must be nodding and considering a discussion on ethics preferable to doing nothing, which exactly was what he'd be doing otherwise.

"All right." Air in. Wheezy breath out.

Eric also smelled minty aftershave wafting through wicker grating. "My daughter," he said, "just turned eight, and she's complaining of being afraid at night. Lots of children are afraid of the boogeyman, one thing or another, but with my daughter, I think it's…different. I believe she's acting this way for attention."

A breath in. Whistling exhalation out. "That's possible. May I ask, do you spend time with your daughter, and by that, I mean do things with her that are meaningful to her?"

Eric thought of the time he'd spent the night before playing cards with Audra, watching television, and said, "Yes." Then he realized last night was the exception and not the rule. "No." A pause. "Maybe."

The tiny bellows of the priest's nose took in air then blew it out. "Then it sounds as though you've already identified the problem. You need only to decide what you mean to do about it."

Eric sighed. The realization that he didn't know what made Audra happy was staggering, and more often than not it was Meredith or Mrs. Mayhew who fixed Audra's meals and looked after her. It was a frightening thing to try to be a father with no roadmap to go by.

He stared at the confessional floor, wishing an easy answer would come, and yet knowing none would.

"You are waiting for some words of comfort?" the priest asked with a wheeze. "Sadly, I haven't any to give." His voice had taken on a strange quality. Tinny. Hollow. "The real sin, my son, is when death occurs as a result of inaction. You do know what I mean by 'inaction'?"

"What?" Eric took his face out of his hands and scrutinized the blackness beyond the wicker screen.

"Wouldn't you agree it would be unfortunate if a child should come to harm because of their parent's absence?"

"I'm not sure I understand —"

Gone was the minty aftershave smell. It had morphed into something else altogether; something pungent and growing stronger by the second.

"How very sad it would be for a child to go hungry or dirty because their parent was too self-involved, too busy to care for them."

"Dirty?"

The smell seeping through the partition was somehow familiar. Like dead fish and rotting vegetables just discovered at the bottom of a bin.

"Un-bathed, unwashed. No one wants their brat stinking like a sow in the high summer sun, do they, Mr. Forshey?"

The smell. The incredible foulness. What the hell was it?

"You *have* been drinking again, haven't you, Mr. Forshey? On the sly? Partaking of the Devil's broth? Tell me, Eric—" (How did the priest know his name?) "—is the coffee you take to work in your thermos each day laced with more than cream? Can you make it through twelve hours without a nip? How long can you go without partaking, anyway? Just between us…six hours? Less?"

The odor was the stink of death. Decay.

"Sin wears many faces, Mr. Forshey."

"Stop…"

"So many, many faces."

"Please…"

"Do you remember the face of your sin, Mr. Forshey?"

"Don't…"

"Why *did* you and your wife divorce? You do remember the last night you were part of a family, don't you?"

Something bubbled to the surface of Eric's consciousness. The priest's words triggered a memory he'd long been suppressing. A memory he didn't want to face because if he did, his mind might snap, might turn on him and slam him down, face to the cold, hard floor of reality, and once there, there would never be any going back.

He remembers. Oh, sweet Jesus, he does. All too clearly, it comes washing over him. A reality he has oh-so-carefully erected comes crashing down like a rain of ice-picks.

He is there all over again. It is a night when he was still married to a beautiful woman with whom he's only grown distant. Meredith is to work late. She asks him to stop and get something for Audra and him to eat.

He picks up cheeseburgers and Cokes at a drive-thru, and when Audra and he finish, she begins her homework.

Becoming restless, he decides to go down to the Langtree Tavern for a couple of frosty ones. Meredith will be home soon. She has some project she's working on at the office but has promised to be home by eight. It will be okay for him to slip off down to the tavern. No problem in that. Audra promises to keep the door locked and the chain in place like she's been taught. Such a good girl, such a bright girl. She will go far, not like her father who never made it beyond the eleventh grade.

He listens to the ceiling-mounted TV as he shoots six games of pool, nurses four beers. He does well, winning all but two games, and after what he considers enough unwind time, he heads home.

When he turns onto his street, however, he sees the ambulances. One is parked in the driveway, the other on the street.

*What the hell?* he thinks. Ambulances can mean only one thing: trouble.

But there can't be any trouble at his house. There just can't be.

Swirling strobes bathe him in red, and the world becomes a foreign, disorienting place.

He pushes past men with medical patches on their jackets. Meredith sits on the coffee table, clutching fistfuls of hair and wailing.

He thunders up the stairs.

Two of the men—the word "paramedics" momentarily escapes him—have his daughter arranged on the linoleum floor. Audra, flat on her back, is not moving. Her lips are blue. One man works feverishly, kneeling in a quarter inch of water, alternately compressing her chest and blowing air into her mouth.

Eric understands. He doesn't want to face facts, but in his mind's eye, he can almost see Audra getting ready for bed.

She steps into the tub.

She slips.

She falls.

Her head makes a sickening crack as it connects with the chromed faucet, the impact of which knocks her unconscious.

Meredith arrives and, seeing Eric's car is missing, lets herself in through the carport side.

Then she makes her discovery, calls 911 before she even shuts off the water.

Yes. He remembers this all.

Now Meredith, back from her perch on the coffee table downstairs, comes up behind him, asking the question which begs asking: "Where were you, Eric? Goddamn it, where were you? WHERE WERE YOU!"

He is too numb to feel the fists pummeling his neck, his arm, his back. Pain does not register to a mind closing off the world, blotting out the shrill and piercing screams. He believes denial will make it somehow less true.

Later, charges of neglect are pressed against him, initiated by Meredith. The charges are summarily dismissed. The court feels the guilt he endures is punishment enough. They are correct.

He and Meredith part bitterly and she relocates out of state.

There is no custody battle because it is never an issue.

His breath hitches deep inside him now, his lungs, near to bursting, seek air. He stumbles from the confessional, gasping.

As suspected, a jerk on the door on the priest's side reveals there is no one there.

The drive home is a collection of jumbled images. The bottle of Scope sliding on the passenger-side floorboard is what he uses to cover up his breath each morning. He doesn't have to remove the cap to recall it smells exactly like the priest's minty aftershave. And the whistle intake and then exhale of the priest's breathing sounds a good deal like the Dodge's asthmatic AC.

The reality he has known is slipping away quickly now. Like a greased rope in a game of tug of war.

On the porch of the duplex, he makes another observation. Mrs. Mayhew has never watched Audra. He knows her name only, because MAYHEW is what is printed on the mailbox just outside her door. He doubts he has spoken two words to her in the time he's lived here.

And upstairs the water is running. Running, and in a distinct way calling for him.

He walks up the stairs, his footfalls leaden.

Then he opens the door to Audra's room—which isn't really Audra's room since she's never actually lived here, has never even seen the inside of *this* place. He looks around at the furniture and toys he's bought secondhand to replicate her old room. He's done a good job, even if he doesn't remember much of it.

The sun is going down, sinking beyond the toothy foothills beyond Chapel Landing. He lies in a fetal position on the bed Audra has never slept in, waiting for nightfall, and when the room is as black as the inside of a confessional, he hears the closet door creak open.

He doesn't need to see to know something with eyes like the slimy whites of raw eggs has entered the room, and when it walks it is with the sound of sludge and sloshing water.

*"Sin wears many faces, Mr. Forshey. So many, many faces."*

The bed is remarkably hard now. The pillow is as resistant as the cold enamel of a claw-foot bathtub. And the rushing of blood in his ears sounds a good deal like running water.

"*Step in here with me, Mr. Forshey,*" he can almost hear it say. "*This will all be over very soon.*"

Eric feels himself being immersed in water, which tightens like a cold band about his chest.

He isn't afraid of Mr. Many Faces, or of the frigid water he brings.

Because if there's one thing Eric Forshey knows, it's that he is ready to accept his contrition.

**S. Clayton Rhodes** is the author of many short stories and is presently working on two novels. His work can be found in such anthologies and periodicals as *Dark Tales of Terror, Startling Stories (Fall 2008 and Winter 2010), New Blood, The Blackness Within, Appalachian Winter Hauntings,* and *Legends of the Mountain State 4,* among others. He currently resides with his wife, Erin, and two daughters, Gabriella and Rachael, in Marietta, Ohio—a town which bears a striking resemblance to the fictional town of Chapel Landing, in which many of his tales are set.

More information can be found at **www.sclaytonrhodes.com**.

# Howling Through the Keyhole

*The stories behind the stories.*

### "Bop Kabala and Communist Jazz"

Partially, this story is based on a visit to my Aunt Sharon's church—one of those charismatic Christian deals—and I found the whole experience surreal. The pastor was wearing Chinese robes and quoting George Carlin's "Stuff" monologue in his sermon. There was a print showing Jesus looking like Dave McKean's version of the Joker holding the world in his hands like a basketball. Another print depicted a nail presumably piercing Jesus' hand—well it was piercing a hand. Everyone was very nice and a few congregants were showing off their Christian tattoos.

However, the main thrust of this story concerns the existential tensions between faith and secularism. As an Orthodox Jew who attends science fiction conventions, I feel just a little out of place in both groups. I am too strange for most of my Jewish friends and among my non-Jewish friends, I am too religious. I've been to science fiction conventions where I've been asked if the yarmulke is a costume. I've been to Shabbos meals where everyone is discussing their camp experiences and their business plans and their jobs and why does there have to be all this sex and violence in the media? Remember that episode of Seinfeld where they end up at a Long Island party and Elaine expresses her boredom by throwing "maybe the dingo ate your baby" lines into conversation? Sometimes it's like that. Ed K. deals with these tensions in one way.

*—Tim Lieder*

### "The Meat Forest"

I often don't know where my story ideas come from—they seem to just appear out of space. This one, though, has a couple of identifiable sources. A few years ago, I saw a documentary on the Gulag, the Russian prison system—the camps, the criminals, and their remarkably intricate and symbolic tattoos. The idea of an escape from a remote prison camp felt like a really compelling germ of a plot, but I couldn't get much past the idea of some guys wandering around the taiga, which didn't seem to make for much drama.

Then, some time later, a Buddhist monk told me that, while he was staying at a monastery in Thailand, one of their daily chants was, "Everything eats." The reason they did this, he said, was to remind themselves of an inescapable aspect of our existence—that eating, consumption, the sacrifice of other beings for our own welfare, is an inherent part of life, that it is impossible to live without causing harm to other beings. I was struck by this image of the universe as a great realm of insatiable hunger, one preying on another, and then in turn being consumed as well. This combined in the bad neighborhoods of my subconscious with the Gulag story, and the meat forest was born.

One of my intentions in writing this (aside from, I hope, entertaining everyone) was to pose this question: In the world of the meat forest, is a life of integrity and compassion possible? Neither the narrator's shallow idealism nor Dmitri's nihilism seem to offer much hope on that front. The Buddhists, I think, would answer yes, but to do so requires us to choose a radically different way of relating to the world. And that is another story entirely.

*–John Haggerty*

### "Drift"

In the fall of 2009, I changed jobs and moved from Pittsburgh to the middle of the state. My new house—a rental, with high Victorian ceilings and "quirks," like ungrounded electrical outlets—was beautiful and much too big for me. And it was cold. So very cold.

Eventually, I realized I couldn't write off the chill as a cold snap, or my unfamiliarity with baseboard electric heaters, or my ridiculous decision to put my desk in the coldest corner of the house. There *was* no warmest corner; the electric heaters just could not keep up with the falling winter. The cold was inescapable, and it was not going away. I spent my evenings huddled under fleece, drinking gallons of hot tea, whining about the temperature on Twitter, often in verse: I'm so very cold / So cold in this house / My fingers are freezing / Right to the mouse. In our most trying circumstances, I think it is important to fight back with doggerel.

So there I was, freezing and thawing regularly, and spending a lot of time writing because once you get nestled into your igloo of a computer chair it's not easy to get up and go ice fishing. Or load the dishwasher. I'd been tossing around different themes and elements lately, trying new things. I wanted to write something about parenthood, something about the shock of realizing an entire generation exists beneath yours, about how strange it is to interact with five-year-olds when you can still remember being five yourself but they have no concept of being thirty. And since I like horror, I wanted to come up with a new and interesting monster.

*Monsters,* I thought. *Parenthood,* I thought. And then, because it was a thing I had been thinking for months in a continual, underlying kind of way: *Cold.*

I put on another scarf, got me some tea, and that's how "Drift" happened.

*–Amanda C. Davis*

### "Worm Central Tonite!"

Squiggly existential carrion-eater stories are a dime a dozen, I know. But far be it from me to resist the latest trend!

*–John Skipp*

### "Fifth Voyage"

"Fifth Voyage" comes out of WCR's impressions of East Tennessee; odd jobs and people he met along the way cropped up in this poem, which unfolded for the first time like a dream. He had to smooth the creases and bridge the gaps both to cover his tracks in the real world and to give readers (without his set of keys) something to latch onto. He dedicates this poem to Lucien Freund, crackpot and crackshot. Go-devil.

*–WC Roberts*

### "Day Job"

When I wrote "Day Job," I was thinking about what it would be like to be a perfect being—an "angel"—and having to spend eternity watching over the flawed, grubby little lives of humans. I'm sure, after a while, even the most perfect being would go a little crazy.

*–Merrilee Faber*

### "A Birth in the Year of the Miracle Plague"

I always wanted to write a zombie story with characters I could care about. For me to care about Joshua (Leper), I had to breathe some life into half of him; and that opened up some doors for him as well as the story.

The idea came to me as I was listening to the song, "Wake Up," by **Arcade Fire**—there was this vision of all these children running rampant through the streets of a tattered city, their parents too broken and afraid to show their faces in daylight. I never intended for the story to be about the Miracle Plague in particular, or its aftermath; I wanted it to be about what the remaining children would do with their time after the world rejected them.

*–Jeremy Kelly*

### "Wanting It"

Every good story carries a sliver of truth. As a boy growing up in a small town in Kansas, I "wanted it" more than anyone. There were many ponds and small, abandoned houses in the countryside around my boyhood home. Once I became an unfettered teenager with a car, the world opened up to me. Mysteries crumbled to dust. The world lost a bit of its spark.

I write to find the magic again. I want to be that little boy.

In my experience, nothing is more horrific than knowing you can never go back, you can never replace innocence once it's lost. I guess that's what "Wanting It" is about. Some things, once gone, are gone forever.

*–Aaron Polson*

### "Eye, You"

It would be nice to say that this story emerged after a deep and complex meditation on how the narcissistic, compulsive exposure of ourselves over the Internet is making our private lives commodities for public consumption. But it didn't. The genesis is much more prosaic—the idea came to me after from watching too much reality TV, mostly *The Osbournes*. Still, I do think the digital conversion of our lives is making us less human, a more consumable product, and may eventually kill us all. And perhaps Google will play an active role in our demise. After all, the popular search engine can be rendered "Go *ogle.*" Coincidence?

*–Joseph Morgado*

### "Stitched"

Normal. I hate that word. It's a judgment, a weapon used by the many against the few. Who or what is normal and what gives them—or us—the right to define it? What if some people really do need to wash their hands six times or dodge the cracks in a sidewalk? If they've convinced themselves that these little rituals hold the world together, do the rest of us benefit from stopping them?

*—Christopher Green*

## "Ruth Across the Sea"

I love writing flash fiction. If ever there's an exercise in brevity then it's producing a story with beginning, middle and end in a thousand words or fewer. "Ruth Across the Sea" is a story of love and loyalty with a medieval feel. It's a tale of self-sacrifice to keep that love alive. It struck me as I was writing that you don't see much lesbianism in medieval fantasy, and there lay the vehicle for the "little twist ending" that flash fiction can thrive upon.

*—Steven Pirie*

## "Duval Street"

I picked up Chuck Palahniuk's *Invisible Monsters* two years ago and I finished it in two days. I remember thinking I want to write something like this, something that screws with people's heads. I've yet to read Fight Club, but I've read enough of his other work to know that Chuck has the "mess with their head then dropkick them in the face" thing mastered. This was my attempt at recreating that feeling, albeit on a much, much smaller scale and with a minor, however forced, steampunk edge.

Why Duval Street?

I have only been to Key West once. It was one of the ports on a week-long cruise my mother and I took almost five years ago. Assuming we weren't missing anything of interest, we remained on the deck and had a late breakfast, watching as other passengers loaded into a trolley with an ancient paint job and squeaky wheels we could hear over the sounds of sea birds and machinery. We made the mistake of waiting until that afternoon to venture out, leaving us with about an hour to gawk at wild parrots and grab a soda from a burger joint off Duval. I remember being amazed that the place had a second floor and seating on the roof. Besides the Japanese staff behind the 24-hour pizza counter on board the ship, and the ridiculous sunburn I acquired in Cozumel, Duval Street was the most memorable part of the trip. I decided that I would return to the island one day, even if only on paper.

This isn't a story about a place so much as it's about the strange people who live there and the stranger things they do when we aren't looking. It's no secret that we all have our quirks. Some of us are better at disguising them while others can't help but flaunt them. And why shouldn't they? But no matter how much time you devote to perfecting your outlandish outward persona, or building your collection of mutant pets from scraps, you will always inevitably be one-upped by someone who's been there, done that, and succeeded ten times over. Stripped down, a special snowflake is still a snowflake. Accept it or refute it, or move to Utah and spread the fever. Either way, let's have drinks.

*—Mekenzie Larsen*

## "Mr. Many Faces"

Every once in a while, a writer's subconscious lends a hand in the creative process. Such is the case with a lot of my work.

When you write fiction often enough, it's my theory you create a relationship with your subconscious, which, at its best, can be a helpful thing. I rather think this was what the ancients referred to when they spoke of artistic muses.

My own subconscious/muse is an important element in my writing. In the best of times, he's like a collaborator, sometimes suggesting interesting storylines and drawing connections I might never have made on my own. Honestly, I love that guy! He can be clever, witty, or downright silly at times. I've laughed out loud at some of the things he's come up with for me to take credit for.

Other times, though, when he is in a particularly grim mood, he grips me by the hand, takes me to a dark place, and reveals something within myself I didn't know was there. "Mr. Many Faces" is the result of such an instance.

Specific to what I meant to achieve, I wanted to do a new riff on the old boogeyman theme. I hoped at least to put my own distinct stamp upon it, and I think I succeeded there.

Choosing to tell the tale with a limited number of characters was a conscious decision (to determine just how limited the cast was, you might actually have to reflect back on the story some more once you've read it, then drop me a line to see if our numbers match). I also knew from the beginning I wanted to keep Mr. Many Faces himself "off screen" as much as possible, if in fact I would show him at all. This is because the best collaborator I could have, next to my subconscious, is you, the reader, and to achieve your full participation, some spaces needed to be left blank for you to fill in.

I hope you enjoyed the ride, or, if you're cheating and reading these little behind-the-scenes notes first, that you *will* enjoy it.

In closing, I'd like to thank Mr. Gary Braunbeck, a fellow author whose work I greatly admire, for kind words of praise when this tale was in its early inception. Thanks also go to Mr. K. Allen Wood and the good people at *Shock Totem* for giving my story a home in the fine publication you now hold in your hands. I can think of no place I'd rather have it.

—S. Clayton Rhodes

**Silent Q Design** was founded in Montreal in 2006 by **Mikio Murakami.** Melding together the use of both realistic templates and surreal imagery, Mikio's artistry proves, at first glance, that a passion for art still is alive, and that no musician, magazine, or venue should suffer from the same bland designs that have been re-hashed over and over.

Mikio's work has been commissioned both locally and internationally, by bands such as **Redemption, Synastry, Starkweather,** and **Epocholypse.** *Shock Totem* is his first book design.

For more info, visit **www.silentqdesign.net.**


**Rex Zachary** has worked in the printing industry for about 10 years as a graphic designer by day and freelance artist at night.

# Shock Totem Submission Guidelines

**What We Want:** We consider original, unpublished stories within the confines of dark fantasy and horror—mystery, suspense, supernatural, morbid humor, fantasy, etc. But the stories must have a clear horror element.

We're interested in journalism, well-researched and emotionally compelling non-fiction about *real* horrors—disease, poverty, addiction, etc.

We're interested in dark poetry on a limited basis.

**What We Do Not Want:** We're not interested in hard science fiction, epic fantasy (swords and sorcery), splatterporn (blood and guts and little more), or clichéd plots. Clichéd *themes* are okay. No fan fiction.

**What We Do Not Want But Will Consider:** Reprints not published within the last 12 months. Author must retain all applicable rights.

**Average Response Time:** 2 months.

**Payment Rates:** We pay 5 cents per word for original, unpublished fiction. We pay 3 cents per word for reprints. There is a $250 cap on all accepted pieces.

**Rights:** We claim First North American Serial Rights and First Electronic World Rights (not to include Internet use) for a period of one year. After which all rights revert to the author.

**For more detailed information, please visit us at
www.shocktotem.com**

Printed in Great Britain
by Amazon.co.uk, Ltd.,
Marston Gate.